TREASURE OF GREEN KNOWE

Treasure of Green Knowe

L. M. BOSTON

Drawings by Peter Boston

A *Voyager/HBJ Book*

HARCOURT BRACE JOVANOVICH

New York and London

Published in England as *The Chimneys of Green Knowe*

Printed in the United States of America

Library of Congress Cataloging in Publication Data

Boston, Lucy Maria, 1892–
Treasure of Green Knowe.

(A Voyager/HBJ book)
SUMMARY: A young boy listens to his great-grandmother's
tales of Green Knowe as it used to be and, gradually, as
past and present blend, he shares the strange adventures of
the former inhabitants.
[1. Space and time—Fiction. 2. England—Fiction]
I. Boston, Peter. II. Title.
[PZ7.B6497Tr 1978]   [Fic]   77-16689
ISBN 0-15-691302-X

First Voyager/HBJ edition 1978
A B C D E F G H I J

To

Jennifer, Helen, Mary, and Dorothy

TREASURE OF GREEN KNOWE

The Easter holidays had begun at last. Tolly bounced up and down on the seat of the railway carriage and looked out of the window. Every hedge and row of elms that sidled past, every stream that the train rumbled hollowly over, each village steeple identified far ahead that grew large and real in its cluster of cottages and trees and slid away again beyond the guard's van was one more landmark passed on the way to the miraculous house of Green Knowe where his great-grandmother lived.

There had been the usual excited babel as the boys poured out of the school bus and raced onto the platform, jostling each other as they lugged cases that were too heavy for them and shouting to their friends to get in with them. The first stage of the journey had been an uproar of joking and singing, in which Tolly, who was a quiet boy, had felt privately that none of the others could really be as excited as he was. They all knew that home would be the same as always, whereas he found himself desperately anxious lest it should be different. He remembered how he had arrived there for the first time only last Christmas, when his father and new stepmother had gone to live in Burma. He had been very lonely—and what entrancing

9

company he had found at Green Knowe! He could hardly believe that his strange companions, Toby, Alexander, and Linnet, had not been people in a dream.

One of the boys, seeing him lost in thought, pulled a lollipop out of his mouth with a plop and said, "It must be dull to stay for the holidays with an old great-grand-mother."

Tolly bobbed up indignantly.

"She lives in a sort of castle—with ghosts," he said.

The other boys had stopped to listen, but on hearing Tolly's answer, they began to pull hideous faces and make wailing and hooting noises and leap upon each other with stiff fingers. Then one of them said, "He's trying to make it sound grand." So Tolly said no more.

After all, it *was* queer—not at all what the boys seemed to think. Much queerer than that. Because (if he could only keep on believing in them) Toby and Alexander and Linnet were the most real and exciting company he had ever had. They belonged to the old house. Anyway his great-grandmother believed in them too. Or had she been playing make-believe with him because he was so little? He became hot with anxiety and his heart was like a runaway steam engine when at last he arrived at Green Knowe again.

First to meet him was his little dog Orlando. Orlando was such an electric commotion it was hard to notice anything else.

Of course the place looked different. He had seen it only in flood, in ice and in snow. This time the wide and

10

wandering garden was silky with daffodils. The cherry trees were coming into blossom and full of birds too busy and independent to hang about waiting for crumbs. The tall stone walls of the house were warming themselves in the sun, and up at the top, under the roof, his own attic window was wide open to welcome him. The river was quiet and reflected huge white clouds.

His great-grandmother, Mrs. Oldknow, was waiting for him at the front door. They hugged each other, and she was little and soft and shaped like a partridge. She was very pleased to see him again and he to see her. She understood what nobody else did. When he was with her, he forgot at once about being a schoolboy. He and she were just two people.

He was in a hurry to go over the house and garden to see that everything was the same, but as soon as he crossed the threshold, he knew that it wasn't. He stood looking at the vases full of spring flowers and the carved cherubs under

11

the ends of the beams, on whose shoulders last year's nests still perched. Orlando kept on barking till the walls re-echoed, so that it was impossible to listen to the house itself —that house where anything might happen and children could play hide and seek from one century into another. But somehow Tolly knew the house was silent. When he had a chance to speak, he turned to his great-grandmother.

"It's different," he said.

"I was afraid you would notice. You're always so quick. But I didn't think you would notice at once. Anyway, lots of things are the same—St. Christopher and the green animals are still there in the garden. Go and look while I get the lunch ready."

Tolly went out with dignity, too proud to run, and renewed his acquaintance with the big statue of St. Christopher against the house wall, wrapped around with new strands of tiny bronze ivy leaves. It impressed him as much as when he had first come across it. It was so very old and weather-worn, such an unexpected thing to be leaning in that friendly, family way against the place where one lived, made of the same stone and sharing the same vines. It stood there gigantic and immovable with stone eyeballs that had been seen but unseeing every since they were carved in the thirteenth century. Tolly felt the statue should receive some greeting from him, but what? He could not think of a proper magic sign that he could make, so he just said its name aloud—St. Christopher. And there was the chaffinch with straw in its beak making a nest in the creepers by the statue's free shoulder.

12

Tolly ran along the track beside the moat under the trees and found the green deer cut out of yew, whose leafy neck he rumpled, and the green hare and the green squirrel and the green peacock. All around them were primroses and moss and sun and shadow, and twigs that had turned brittle in the winter crackled gaily under his feet. When he had finished his tour of inspection, he went into the house and stopped opposite the big open hearth. The fire was burning cheerfully, but over the beam on the rather smoky wall was a large clean patch where previously the oil painting of the Oldknow family had hung. The space was partly covered up by a smaller picture that Tolly could not bother even to look at.

"*Where have they gone?*" he said accusingly to Mrs. Oldknow. "Toby and Alexander and Linnet—where are they? Why have you put up that thing there instead of them?"

"Their portrait has gone to an exhibition in London. People who have old pictures are often asked to lend them. I knew you would be sorry, but I didn't like to refuse."

"How long will it be there?"

"The exhibition lasts six weeks." She sounded so uncertain that Tolly insisted on an answer.

"Will they be back then? When it's over?"

"I have been wondering, Tolly, whether I ought not to take the opportunity, when so many people are admiring it, to sell the picture."

"You can't do that!" Tolly was beside himself. "You

13

can't sell them. They must be here. You can't sell Toby and Alexander and Linnet." He was nearly in tears.

"I know, my dear. Oh, I know. But I have so little money and the roof leaked everywhere after the thaw. The place will rot away if I don't put it right."

"You can't sell them. Think, Granny. They would hang somewhere else where they didn't belong. They would have nowhere to *be*." Tolly could imagine nothing more dreadful. "They'd rather be here, even if the roof fell in. I don't believe they'd mind at all about the roof."

"I don't think they would either." She smiled at him. "And the mouse would just love a ruin. But you know the house will be yours, and I hope your children's too. It mustn't fall down."

"I'd rather have it a ruin and them still here." Tolly minded more and more as he thought of it.

"Even if we didn't mind lying in bed with water dripping on us, we wouldn't be allowed to do it. Green Knowe is an ancient monument, and I'm obliged by law to keep it in order."

"Can't you sell something else?"

"I've nothing else really valuable. It's not as though there were any jewels still in the family. I would gladly have sold all those and they'd never have been missed, but they were lost long ago."

"Whose jewels?"

"Hers," said the old lady wearily, pointing to the picture that had taken the place of Toby, Alexander, and

14

Linnet. Tolly looked at it. It showed a very fashionable lady being driven in a high springy carriage with four white horses toward a mansion. They were approaching a small bridge across some water that apparently surrounded the house. It looked somehow familiar and yet was nowhere that Tolly recognized.

"Who is she?" he asked.

"Maria Oldknow, the wife of Captain Oldknow, who was in the Royal Navy. It ran in the family. The men all went to sea. There she is, driving back from a party the very day the jewels disappeared in 1798."

"Didn't she live here?"

"Oh, yes. But before she would marry the Captain, he had to build a much grander house for her. You may laugh, but that big house in the picture has got this one inside it! You can see our chimney sticking out of the top. Of course, all the best rooms were in the new building, so our part was left for the children and the old Nanny, and the servants. Then later there was a fire and all the new part was burnt down and only our part with its thick stone walls was left."

"Were the jewels stolen?"

"Nobody ever found out."

Tolly spent the afternoon in the garden, where he found Boggis, the gardener, but nobody else. He had Orlando to play with, and Orlando found the hedgehog rolled up under a heap of leaves. This roused Tolly's hopes for a while, but soon it was achingly clear that his former

15

playfellows were absent. He could feel that they were gone quite out of reach. He came in sadly at sunset. After looking forward to it for so long, the first day of the holidays seemed as flat as an empty Christmas stocking.

His great-grandmother was sitting by the fire mending one of the old patchwork quilts. Tolly had long been familiar with the quilts, some of which were used as curtains in the living room, hanging from ceiling to floor in bulgy folds against the stone walls. Spread across her knees and rucked up round her on the floor, they were both more intimate and more intriguing. The colors and patterns were so lively in the firelight that Tolly at once sat down to enjoy them. Mrs. Oldknow had a basket beside her full of pieces of paper all cut the same size and shape, over which she had neatly tacked bright cotton materials. These she was trying on over torn pieces in the quilt to see which looked best.

"Blue stars or scarlet ferns?" she asked Tolly, trying first one and then the other.

"Scarlet ferns I think."

"So do I. But I hate covering up the old bits. It's like burying something that perhaps needn't be dead. So I never do it till the old piece has quite, quite gone. Look! On this patch someone wrote in India ink *1801*. The quilt was made in this house, and all the pieces are from the clothes of the people who still lived here in 1801, their clothes and their curtains. Mostly her clothes," she said,

16

jerking her head toward the picture of the lady in the
four-horse carriage. "She had so many. She was a vain and
silly woman. This ragged piece"—the old lady jabbed at
it with her finger—"was one of her best Indian muslins.
Yellow as a canary when it was new and as fine as gossamer.
I must say they were lovely things. Look, here's a piece of
the same that hasn't gone to holes yet. Feel it with your
finger. What have you ever felt that was as soft?" Tolly
fingered it and thought.

"Dandelion clocks," he said.

"Dandelion clocks! And she liked to imagine *she* was
the most delicate thing that ever happened. It wasn't her
fault if her hands weren't softer than her muslins. Let's
play at detectives. See what other people you can find
in this patchwork. There're all sorts."

"Well, there would be a father, I suppose. Here's a bit

17

of shirt, but it's rather thick. It would do for Boggis—if there was a Boggis then."

"There was indeed."

"Here's a nicer piece for the father."

"Well done. What else can you find?"

"There ought to be some children." Tolly searched in the patchwork folds. "Boggis did have a lot of shirts."

"He wasn't the only servant. There was, for instance, the footman. Here's his yellow-and-black-striped apron that he wore while he polished the silver and brasses."

"What nasty stuff! Like a wasp."

"He was a nasty man."

"There's nothing at all like anything Linnet wore."

"Don't look for Linnet. This is a hundred and fifty years after she lived. Little girls were dressed just like their mothers only smaller, in long tight dresses."

"I don't know what girls have," said Tolly impatiently. "I'll do it by magic."

"Detectives don't use magic."

"Water diviners do. I'll spread my hands out and wave them over the patchwork and when a finger tickles, that's it."

Tolly fixed his face into a long-lipped solemnity that he thought suitable for water diviners, and with closed eyes he passed his fingers slowly and hesitantly over the quilt.

"What's her name?" he asked without stopping the play of his hands.

"Susan."

"Susan, Susan, Susan, this is Tolly calling. Susan, where are you? Over to you, Susan."

His finger came down on a patch, and he opened his eyes. His great-grandmother bent down to look.

"Quite right! Not her clothes, but you've hit on her bed curtains. All beds used to have curtains at the head like babies' cots, only for grownups. And some were like tents. Susan's was."

"I'd like a tent bed."

"Well, once inside you were private, but stuffy."

"Do you think Susan really pulled my finger onto the right stuff?"

"No. I think it was someone else. Someone who liked magic as much as you do."

"Who else was there?"

"Find out for yourself. They are all here."

"There's lots of black with white and purple patterns. I suppose that's the grandmother. Did she like magic?"

"She did not. Nobody disliked it so much. She thought it very, very wicked."

"Well, who then?"

But Mrs. Oldknow only sewed and smiled.

"Who would wear bright emerald green and scarlet, almost as thick as school sheets?" asked Tolly.

"Now you are getting warm. Somebody who hated them, poor lamb."

"Was it Susan's brother?"

"Sefton? No. He didn't have to put up with anything he disliked. He was very handsome, like his mother, and

19

she gave him everything he wanted. Look, here's a bit of his shirt, finer than his father's. And here's his printed dressing gown for lounging about in his mother's bedroom, where he used to talk scandal, telling tales and making her laugh. Here's his riding coat, chestnut twill. It had a primrose lining. His hair was chestnut too, and when he went hunting, he used to say he was King Fox."

"He doesn't sound as nice as Toby."

"Not nearly as nice. But you won't meet him here. He thought nothing of the place."

"Do you mean I might meet someone else?"

"You might, if you listen to the house and try to catch it when it doesn't know you're looking. It's full of secrets. You know that."

"I shan't like anybody as much as Toby and Alexander and Linnet. But perhaps I'll hear thieves saying where the jewels are, and then we can have the picture back for always and they'll come home."

That evening Tolly was glad to be back in his own bedroom under the roof. In the Christmas holidays icicles had hung in a fringe over the windows, but now they were open to the warm spring winds, and as he leaned out, he could see a long stretch of river winding in each direction and it was pink in the sunset. Tolly had wanted Orlando to sleep with him, but while he had been away at school, Orlando had chosen an armchair in the living room that exactly fitted him, with the arm just right for resting his chin on, and he preferred to stay there.

Tolly pleaded with him, but he closed his eyes and was deaf, smiling in perfect comfort.

When Tolly got into bed and drew his own patchwork quilt up to his chin, he noticed that a great many pieces were of the same materials that he had seen downstairs across his great-grandmother's knees.

"There are bits of those people everywhere," he thought. It seemed queer to him that he had never even wondered about the quilt before. Mrs. Oldknow came up to say good night to him and sat down on the bed.

"My quilt has lots of the same pieces in it as yours."

"Yours was Susan's quilt. The grandmother made them all. She did almost nothing but sit and sew patchworks and look severe. She really liked doing it better than anything else, but she thought it wicked to enjoy anything. When her daughter-in-law Maria refused to have one for her own bed, preferring satin and lace, the grandmother was very angry and said huffily, 'Then little Susan shall have it for when she is married.' 'Susan married indeed!' said Sefton, the brother. 'That's a good joke!' Maria said Susan was hardly likely to get an offer of marriage, but if Granny liked to go on making patchworks, Susan could have them in bundles of a dozen. Susan wouldn't mind how old-fashioned anything was."

"How rude she was."

"She and the grandmother didn't get on at all well. Maria and Sefton and Susan were all disappointments to the old lady."

Tolly's thoughts were wandering.

21

"When I told the boys at school that you lived in a sort of castle with ghosts, they didn't believe me."

"Ghosts! What a thing to call them."

"What do you call them?"

"The others."

"I like this house. It's like living in a book that keeps coming true."

In the morning the first thing he saw was the old rocking horse standing there quite still as if it had fallen into a trance until some other child should come and wake it. He had outgrown it. At school he was learning to ride real horses. They were not, alas, at all like Feste, Toby's horse. Their coats were not shining silk but rough like railway upholstery, and when one patted them, clouds of dust came out. They were bony and their feet were large, and all their movements were reluctant. They were tired of teaching people to ride, and all pupils were the same to them. Tolly had to pretend on one of them almost as much as on the rocking horse. He longed for a horse that pranced and could not wait to be off. Some day that would happen. After all, he was still only nine.

He got out of bed to see what kind of day it was going to be. His window was so high that he saw the garden lying far below the sky, laid out tidily like a toy model. Across the lawn a little black and white dog was running about, legs moving like clockwork. Tolly watched to see what Orlando would do by himself. He was an endearing creature full of amusing ways. He was doubling back and forth full tilt across the garden following the scent of some animal that had been there in the night but was there no longer. He's pretending it's still there, thought Tolly. Suddenly Orlando broke off and ran to the gate, jumping up and dancing around as if a friend of his had just come in. Tolly watched him, fascinated. "Can he really be pretending I've just come home? While I was away did he play that I came back?" Orlando accompanied his imaginary friend all the way to the house. Then Tolly leaned out and called, and in a very short time heard a scamper up the steep stairs.

At breakfast Tolly told Mrs. Oldknow about this, but she did not seem to be listening, because she only answered, "I expect he made friends with someone while you were away."

"But there wasn't anyone there, Granny."

"Wasn't there? I never heard of dogs pretending that way. I don't believe they do."

Tolly spent the morning being a detective looking for hidden jewels. He went round the house tapping the walls to see if there were hollow places in the stone, especially at the back of cupboards, and looking at the floor boards to see if there were boards that had been cut short and screwed back again. It was a good game, but he did not find anything. Orlando went with him, a keen assistant who was always in the way, always first, always underneath him, blowing down cracks and barking whenever a cupboard door was not opened quickly enough.

23

Tolly asked his great-grandmother if he could look in her room, and she said yes, if he left everything as he found it. Orlando ran ahead up the stairs, and when Tolly followed him into Mrs. Oldknow's bedroom, he caught him at his tricks again, wagging at someone who wasn't there, but if someone had been there, he or she would seem to be sitting in a child's armchair that Mrs. Oldknow kept there. In this room there were window seats in the recesses under the big windows, with cushions on the seats and a wooden front below them that sounded hollow when tapped. Tolly looked in the wooden panel for signs of a door that might have lost its knob or perhaps a drawer that would pull out, but the front was solid. He pulled off the cushion and examined the seat. Orlando stood on his hind legs and blew in rhythmic puffs under the ledge. Sure enough, it was a lid, but it had not been opened for so long that Tolly could not move it. However, at last as he heaved with all his might, it came up with a protesting squawk. Inside was a large linen bag full of bits and pieces that were now familiar to him from the patchwork: a doll's patchwork quilt made to scale and a battered wooden doll that Orlando seized and went off with, shaking it like a rat and lovingly chewing it like a bone. Tolly should perhaps have stopped him, but he had found a small wooden ship, apparently hand-carved, very elaborate, with a long bowsprit and three masts. The name *Woodpecker* was painted on the bows. It was an unexpected shape, low in the bows and high in the stern, but not at all clumsy like a galleon. He felt its lines, weighed it in his hands, and

24

knew that it would ride the water well. He took a great fancy to it and longed to ask Mrs. Oldknow if he could keep it. It had its sails, but the main mast was broken and the rigging torn, as if someone had trodden on it. With patience it could be mended.

He laid the ship aside for the moment, and, plunging his hands into the litter of old curtains under the window seat, he felt fur and then—boxes! Perhaps these were the jewels. He hauled them out a flat leather box with a silver clasp and a large polished wooden box with a brass square inlaid on the lid, on which was engraved in Roman letters, quite one inch high and widely spaced, the name SUSAN OLDKNOW. There were two other boxes, but Tolly opened the most important-looking first. His hands were almost violent with excitement. The leather box contained a necklace and bracelet of coral beads twisted into a fascinating rope pattern, each lying in a satin socket. They were very pretty, but Tolly thought coral was never mentioned in Aladdin's cave and wasn't perhaps worth a fortune. The real jewels must be in the big box. But why Susan Oldknow? It should be Maria. The box was not locked, and Tolly would have been bitterly disappointed on opening it if its contents had not been so immediately enchanting. It was filled with beautifully fitted trays, and as each was lifted out, there was another underneath. In the first were shells of every kind laid out in rows on wadding—fanlike or spiral or curly, mother of pearl, rose petal, or crisp, heavy, or featherweight. Each was a pleasure to touch. Some were so small as to slip into the cracks between his fingers. He arranged them all as he found them and went on to the next tray. This held pebbles—moonstone, amber, agate, quartz, alabaster, marble, or slate—all worn to their perfect shape as the sea rolls them, exciting to handle, some slippery, some eggshell, some pulling on the finger like glass paper, some cold, some warm. There were four trays in all, each filled with treasures of the sea, brittle dry seaweed, starfish, sea urchins, crystals growing like plants, branches of natural coral. Tolly had been to the sea only once, where it pounded on the shingle by a promenade. But he had read *Coral Island*. He knew now that he had not found Maria's jewels, so there was no hurry. He spent a long time handling the collection. He could never guess what each piece would weigh. Some, like cowrie shells, were unexpectedly heavy—he popped one into his mouth to "taste" the shape—others were so light he had to hold his breath while he picked them up, or to lick his finger so that they would stick to the end.

Of the remaining boxes one contained beads of all shapes and sizes, glass, ivory, china, blue stone, and cedarwood—these with a delicate fruity scent.

The last box was carved all over with an intricate pattern of lines like intersecting waves. In the center of the lid all the lines drew together into the rays of a round sun, and in the center of the sun was an S. Tolly traced the S with his fingertip while he thought. This looked to him like some sort of magical sign. His great-grandmother had said *somebody* liked magic. Somebody who wore bright red and green. Somebody of whom till now he had found no trace. Inside this box there was a medley of fir cones,

26

conkers, acorns, the little wooden flowers that are left when the beechnut drops out, feathers, fossils, glass marbles, a peg top, a cut-glass bottle stopper, a knight out of a chess set. These were all things you might expect to find in any boy's pocket. In fact, he recognized with surprise, all the things he had found were finger pleasures—things you turned over in your hand and mind without looking at them.

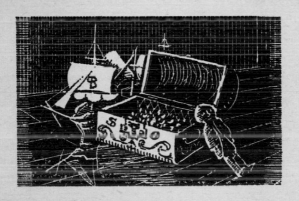

Tolly now thought that, though he had found no jewels, he was being rather clever as a detective, especially when, as he was carrying the toy ship away to show Mrs. Oldknow, the sun struck into a corner of her room and showed a small picture he had not noticed before of a sailing ship in a storm. Underneath it was printed:

The frigate "Woodpecker" in the Great Gale of 1797 off Teneriffe

He started off helter-skelter to tell Mrs. Oldknow what he had found, but on the stairs he remembered he ought to leave her room tidy and put the cushion back on the window seat, so he turned round and went back. As he came through the door, he nearly bumped into a girl who was standing in the other doorway leading to the music room. She was about his own age, with large soft brown eyes. She was in dressing-up clothes, and perhaps that explained her startled and hesitant manner, but she held her ground, and it was she who spoke first.

"Who's there?" she said, staring at him.

"I'm Tolly."

"Tolly?"

"Toseland, if you like it better."

"Oh. I didn't know the cousins were coming. I had better change my dress. Will you tell Granny I am coming as soon as I can?"

She walked cautiously across the room as if she were listening and put out a hand that found of its own accord the embroidered strap of the old pull bell that hung by the bed. Tolly heard it ring and ran downstairs, making an excuse to himself that he wanted to be in time to find the bell while it was still swinging. He had a funny feeling that, though he was coming down, sliding half over the banisters, there was a sound of footsteps *going up.*

His great-grandmother was waiting for him at the bottom. He stood panting and holding the boat behind him and couldn't say anything.

"So you've met Susan," she said.

"How did you know?"

"No one but Susan ever rings that bell."

"I could have rung it."

"No you couldn't. Come here and see."

She led him to the kitchen wall where, under the ceiling, a set of wires was attached to a row of bell hooks, but the bells had all been taken off. It seemed to Tolly that one of the wires was trembling.

"I have an electric bell now," she said, "but I left the embroidered strap there because I like it. Besides there are not many of Susan's things here."

"Did you know about this?"

Tolly held out the boat.

"The *Woodpecker*!"

"I know. In the great gale of 1797 off Teneriffe!" Tolly began to laugh and jump up and down, but Mrs. Oldknow was serious, as if she couldn't believe her eyes.

"Where did you find that?"

"In your room. Didn't you know Susan's toy box was there?"

"No. Where?"

"Her toys and the bits the patchwork was made of, and lots of boxes of things."

They went up together. The lid screeched open again, and there lay all the boxes on top of the linen bag. Mrs. Oldknow traced with her fingers the wide-spaced letters engraved on the box and seemed far away in thought.

"To think how often I have sat there sewing in the

summer and even mending the patchwork, and all the time all these things were there! The beginning and the end so near together, like a telescope when you shut it up."

"What's this fur?"

"Why, it's the grandmother's foot muff that Sefton gave her."

"You mean King Fox?"

The foot muff was made of a fox skin, stuffed and curled round like a dog asleep.

"You put your feet where it puts its own nose, under its stomach, where there is lining of sheepskin, and there you are, as warm as toast. . . . Just what I want for the winter. She always sat with her feet in it while she was sewing, and so shall I."

"Good thing Orlando didn't find that."

"Where is Orlando? I thought he was with you."

"He was, but—oh dear! He was munching an old doll. A horrid old wooden thing. I hope you don't mind. Perhaps he's still got it. I'll go and look."

Tolly found Orlando sitting wagging at the foot of the beech tree, looking up into the branches as though he had chased a cat up there and was going to wait until it came down if it took days. Tolly could not see any cat, or anything else, but he did notice that it would be an excellent tree to climb. If you had a good head for height, you could get right to the top. He did not know if he had a good head, for he had never been up so high, but he determined to try. Meanwhile, he dragged Orlando indoors by the collar, and on the way stumbled on the wooden

30

doll, sucked, splintered, and marked with toothholes, but still recognizable.

❦

"Now tell me about Susan," Tolly said later as they settled down by the fire, which was only made up into a blaze in the evenings now, when the firelight and the sunset crossed each other in the room and every polished surface that could twinkle shone double. Mrs. Oldknow did not light any lamps because they were only going to talk; and while she talked, Tolly watched the shadows moving and the reflection of the flames in the windowpane, where it looked as if the yew tree was on fire.

"There was something about Susan," he began, "that was different from Linnet. She stood there looking at me as if I wasn't there. It made *me* feel as if I was—one of *the others*. I wanted to find you to make sure that I wasn't."

"I expect you were very real to her, as real as anybody else. You see, she was blind."

"Do you mean she couldn't see me?"

"She was quite blind."

"But she walked about like anybody else."

"So did Linnet's dear Truepenny, the Mole."

❧ THE STORY OF SUSAN ❧

What is really hard to believe is that her mother and old Nanny Softly did everything they possibly could to keep

Susan from learning to find her way about. When they first discovered she was blind—and no one could tell by looking at her—there was great weeping and wailing.

Maria's cry of despair was, "Whatever shall I do with a blind daughter—I can't take her into society—she'll never be married—there will be no pleasure in dressing her—she won't even be able to dress herself and we'll have her for *always*." At this point Maria had the vapors and had to be put to bed.

The grandmother said it was a judgment on Maria for her flighty life, and though the child would be little more than an idiot, she would try to see that it was at least a Christian one.

Sefton, who was already ten years old when Susan was born, spoilt by his mother and ready to be furiously jealous of another child, privately thought the whole arrangement—a mere girl and blind at that—was quite satisfactory.

Nanny Softly rocked and wept and clasped the child to her featherbed bosom and said at least the poor little thing shouldn't be without someone to love her. What bumps her poor dear little head was going to get! But she would watch her day and night and never let her out of her sight. Her old Nanny Softly would always be with her. This was really a far worse threat for Susan than Maria's indifference, because though it was good for her to be loved, it was dreadful never to be allowed to try to do anything herself. She was an active, intelligent little person full of curiosity. She wanted to crawl, to walk, to explore, to find out where people vanished to, to touch and handle everything and learn what things were and where they could be found again.

Nanny Softly was as good as her word, kind stupid woman, and wouldn't let her alone. Let Nanny do it, Nanny will fetch it, Nanny will button it, Nanny will tie it, Nanny will feed you, Nanny will wash your hands. Anything Susan wanted to try for herself she had to do quickly while Nanny wasn't there. Once Nanny caught her warming her own hands by the fire, and once actually standing at the top of the stairs, and she let out a scream that Susan would fall and kill herself and carried her away and strapped her in a chair. After that Susan lived strapped in a chair, except when she sat a prisoner on Nanny's knee, or somebody led her by the hand. In leading her, they were impatient, because their idea was to get her quickly where they were going, while Susan's idea was to feel everything possible on the way there. Everything was to her most mysterious, because she only felt a bit of it as she was dragged past, a ledge or a knob, a fold of curtain, or perhaps she felt nothing, but there was a different smell or a hollower sound. She had no idea how big things were or what shape. They stuck out of space like icebergs out of the sea. For this reason she enjoyed the continuous pleasantly shaped stair rail and liked to draw her fingers along the banisters as she went up and down, pushed and pulled by Nanny Softly.

("Like a tied-up dog," said Tolly sadly, thinking of Orlando and perfectly understanding.)

Very soon Susan began to resent Nanny, who fussed her and thwarted her and captured her hands and held them while the cup was put to her lips, because she might spill it, and wiped her mouth for her, and slapped her hands when they fingered things of great interest, such as frills being ironed. There were battles and tempers, and the punishment was to be strapped in her chair again and left there. And there she sat for hours, with her wooden doll tied to the arm by a string, so that if she dropped it, Nanny did not have to get up and give it to her. But who wants a toy that is tied to her? However, it was a wooden doll, as you have seen, and she could hit out nicely with it, and once Nanny Softly caught a good rap over the head. Then she threatened to burn the doll. As if Susan cared!

Old Mrs. Softly was a great talker, and all the household came up to the nursery to gossip with her, including of course the manservant Caxton, who wore the wasp-colored apron, the gardener Boggis, and Sefton when he wanted something done for his convenience or a little lie told to his father to ward off a punishment, or merely to boast to his old nanny, who believed everything he said and always told him he was handsomer and more manly from day to day. He liked to hear it and had for her a specially wheedling voice.

"Nanny, you old dragon, I suppose you wouldn't do something for me just for once?"

34

"How can you call me such a thing, Master Sefton! As if I didn't always spoil you."

"Spoil me! You were so strict I went in fear of my life. You're the only person I've ever been afraid of." Nanny purred with pride at this nonsensical flattery.

"Anyway, Master Sefton, I'm proud of the result. You do me credit. What was it you wanted?"

"Well, listen, Nanny. The groom says there's a peep show at St. Neots of the French King having his head cut off! The crowds shout just as if it was real. You can hardly get in. I can't miss a thing like that, can I? I'm taking the groom and will probably be back late, because if anybody cheers when the King dies, there's a free fight, and I must be there for that. So tell my father I've gone to the field day of the county militiamen. We have a lot a secrets together, don't we, Nanny! There's a kiss for you."

All these talkers behaved freely, as though Susan, because she couldn't see them, couldn't hear them either, or at least did not count. But Susan heard far more than other people and understood it better too. She had nothing to do but listen—hers was a world of voices. Voices did not deceive her, and she could not see the smiles that were meant to deceive. She knew at once what people really meant, what they thought of the person they were speaking to, and even what they didn't say. Caxton she feared and hated. When her mother or father were present, he would pinch her cheek and talk baby talk, but when only Mrs. Softly was there, he would say, "It should have been drowned like a kitten." By the time Susan was your age she knew everybody's secrets. Sefton and Caxton had a great many, concerned with betting, cock-fighting, bear-baiting, dicing, and worse.

One of Susan's treats was being taken to visit her mother before she was put to bed. Maria had a low-pitched, pleasure-loving voice, and she laughed very easily and charmingly, though not always kindly. To her daughter she was someone whose room had special softnesses and special smells. Even the way she said "Come in" when Susan knocked—that at least Nanny Softly let her do for herself—made it sound like a special favor to be allowed in. Then a cool hand would be put out to take her from Nanny, and with it came a whiff of Maria's own scent. The hand had rings on it and the wrist wore jingling bracelets and the arm was generally warm and bare. If the dress or wrap was not too precious to be crushed, Susan was allowed to sit on her mother's knee, and because Maria enjoyed being loved, Susan was allowed to feel with her hands the smooth shoulders and neck, and round the chin up to the face. Then Maria would say, "And where is Mama's nose? And where are Mama's eyelashes (they were very long) and where are Mama's dimples?" And Susan would put her finger on each in turn. Then there were her clothes made of the finest materials, and her fur or swansdown wraps. Though Maria always spoke of "My saffron muslin" or "my mulberry velvet," Susan recognized them by the feel alone. Nearly every evening they did the same thing. Maria brought out her jewel box, and Susan was allowed

36

to choose what should be worn and to clasp it round her mother's neck or slip it onto her wrist. The earrings of course were among the difficult things that it was beyond her power to put on , though she might touch them gently when they were in place. She was allowed to let the string of pearls run through her fingers or the diamonds lie in her palm. She loved the pearls, and anything like filigree or twisted gold chains or lockets on velvet ribbon or rings; but she could not imagine why diamonds were so precious. They were hard, heavy, edgy, and cold. However, she had no difficulty in believing that this wearing of very special things round one's neck or wrist or fingers was most important and made her mother different from other people and superior to them. Her private belief was that the jewels were charms. She had heard Nanny talk about the Evil Eye, and to someone who can't imagine what "seeing" can possibly mean, the Evil Eye is as dreadful as it is vague.

Maria never let Susan wear any of the jewels herself, beyond slipping her little hand through a bracelet, and that was soon taken away lest she should drop it. Neither Maria nor Mrs. Softly seemed to realize that Susan never dropped anything. Because she did not seem as anxious as they thought she ought to be about dropping things, they thought she was careless.

Sometimes Maria was in a more than usually idle good temper and let Susan play a long time and sang to her and made her sing. Sometimes she would suddenly get tired of her before the jewels were even back in their cases, and call for Nanny Softly saying, "You can take Susan. I've had enough of her for tonight." Susan would hardly be allowed to press the clasp of a lid together before she was hauled away, leaving behind her all the fascinating leather boxes, oval, or oblong, or domed to take a high bracelet, each box scented and lined in silk or velvet, with a notch that exactly fitted what was to lie there and a satisfactory snap when the lid was closed. It was like being dragged from heaven. Her lingering fingers pinched the lace ruffles round the dressing table, but Nanny Softly was relentless.

"Come along now, Miss Susan. How often have I told you fingering is bad manners."

Sometimes, but not nearly often enough, her father was at home, on leave between one voyage and the next. He loved his daughter very deeply. Her blindness seemed to him not a defect but a mysterious charm. It tore his heart to see how stupidly Maria and Mrs. Softly treated her, how they forced her to be helpless when all the time she was eager and curious and self-confident. Every time he came home, it struck him afresh. Sometimes he was away for a year, in which time Sefton would have grown noticeably more independent and willful, but the only change in Susan was that each time he went away she minded more. He did not know what to do for her. In those days nobody had heard of Braille and there were no schools for the blind. If they were poor, they had to be beggars. If rich, they were prisoners with servants. Captain Oldknow could tell by his love for Susan that their treatment of her was as wrong as it was unnecessary.

"Let her finger it, Mrs. Softly. There is no hurry. How do you expect her to know about things?"

"I am sorry, sir. I do the best I can, I'm sure. And sometimes those that are always with a child know best. If I didn't check her, she would be fingering everything all the time. There's nothing harder to teach her. Her fingers would be in the fire, in the coal, and the syrup. Everything would be broken or lost. I wouldn't put it past her to steal. Do you know what I found under her mattress the other day? One of her mother's gold bracelets. Now don't you go encouraging her to finger, please, sir. It's hard enough to bring her up as it is."

"Don't use hard words like stealing, Mrs. Softly. My little girl doesn't steal. She just wanted something of her mother's to take to bed with her. Come and say good night to your father, Susan. Would you like something of mine to take to bed with you tonight? How about my watch?" He took his gold watch off the fob on which it hung and all his seals and keys and gave them into Susan's hands. She knew how to press the watch so that it struck the hours and minutes. She went to bed immensely proud and happy.

"Couldn't you even kiss her good night?" he said bitterly to his wife after Susan had gone.

"No I couldn't. I think mothers and daughters kissing each other is horridly vulgar. Nanny Softly kisses her enough. She absolutely gobbles her if that's what you want. I have her in here and make a fuss of her every night, and however much you criticize me, the child dotes on her mother. You must admit it."

"I do admit it. I would rather it was the other way round. Nanny Softly is an ignorant old woman. You ought to teach Susan and help her to do things for herself."

"You'd need the patience of an angel. And how would I find time? Even Nanny says she would weary a growing tree." Maria put her head back and laughed with a soft gurgle. "What an expression! Anyway her grandmother teaches her religion."

"My mother is very strict. She seems to me to make Susan suffer for the fact that Sefton is so much indulged."

"Ah! Sefton can do nothing right in your eyes. It is you, my dear husband, who crab Sefton just because he can't help enjoying life better than a blind sister."

Captain Oldknow sighed like a ship in a trough and went away to pace up and down his study. When he was at home, he spent as much time as he possibly could with Susan, taking her on walks, telling her stories, and trying to invent games they could play together in his study. Hide and seek was one, in which he always was the hider and she must make her way alone about the room to find him. In this way his study became a place where she was confident and independent, far more so than in her nursery, for the Captain insisted on everything being kept in its own place, whereas when Nanny cleared up, she put everything where it had never been before.

On her father's knee Susan heard stories of the sea and of lands on the other side of it. When she asked, "What is the sea?" he said that it was water like the bath but as big as half the world.

"As big as we walked this afternoon?"

"Far bigger. And the ships floating on it may be as big as houses."

"What does float mean?"

"What sticks do down the river."

"I don't know what they do," said Susan, who was not afraid of telling her father what she didn't know. "Nanny Softly took me for a walk by the river, and I asked her to let me feel it, but she said that was silly, you can't feel rivers. And she said I mustn't go near or I'd be drowned. Does a river come up and snatch you?"

Try as he might to imagine not ever seeing anything, the Captain was always being surprised.

As a result of this conversation, the next time he came home he brought her two big spiky shells in which, when she held them over her ears, she could hear the sound of the breakers, water running over running water. He brought her too a model of his own frigate, *Woodpecker*, to float in her bath where she could make waves with her legs and feel how the boat tossed, and blow on the sails and feel the keel move forward between her palms, so that, when he was away, she could imagine the gales and the fair weather. Susan so loved the *Woodpecker* she wanted a bath every night. But in those days there were no bathrooms. Tin baths were carried into the bedrooms with jugs of hot water; and if carrying them in was a nuisance, emptying them out was still worse, a matter of

41

heaving and spilling, which made Mrs. Softly puff and blow. Once a fortnight had been considered enough. But Susan was so passionately attached to the *Woodpecker* that the old woman gave way to her.

"There now! What fancies children do get. If it was a boy, I'd understand. But what can she know about ships, poor lamb. And me toiling up and down with hot water."

Susan was seven when she was given the *Woodpecker*, and her father was home on a very short visit. It was while he was reciting to her the *Ballad of Lord Bateman* that he thought of the parson's son Jonathan, who was the same age as Sefton, seventeen. The two boys had known each other all their lives and had been educated together by the parson, Mr. Morley, until Sefton went to school. They never wanted each other's company as small boys or in after years as neighbors, though Jonathan rode and shot quite as well as Sefton, even better. Sefton was reckless and had ruined two of his father's best horses. Captain Oldknow had to admit that his son was irresponsible and inconsiderate and often arrogant. For this reason he hesitated to offer Jonathan, who was reserved and likeable, a position in his house where Sefton might treat him as an underling. In the end, for Susan's sake, he asked Jonathan to come in every morning to teach Susan by reading to her and telling her classical stories. He felt sure he could teach her a great deal himself but did not know how to explain to Jonathan, who went red with embarrassment at the thought.

"How can I teach her anything if she can't read or write? Where do I begin?"

"Use your brains! You begin by word of mouth," said the Captain with unusual sharpness, "and you answer *all* her questions and make sure she understands the answers. And keep on reminding yourself that the one thing she *isn't* is stupid. Above all, whatever you do, make it a pleasure. Give her something to think about, something to look forward to. Here's a list of books to start with. *Robinson Crusoe, Hakluyt's Voyages, Gulliver's Travels.* She likes learning by heart. Read her ballads. She'll learn them more quickly than you do. Anything with a lilt. Your father is one of my oldest and most valued friends. If you succeed in doing what I want for Susan, you will double the bond between our families and I shall be grateful."

All the same, as he searched with his authoritative sea-going eyes Jonathan's face, half-boy, half-man, and remembered that he had no sisters of his own, Captain Oldknow wondered how it would work. Susan at least would not see her tutor's blushes.

Jonathan came next day to begin his duties.

"I hear you have been given the job of confidential nursery governess," said Sefton at the front door, laughing with full use of his good looks, one foot in the stirrup as his horse danced round. "My compliments! I'd sooner be training a horse or a dog myself."

Sefton's voice, like his mother's, was full of laughter and well-being. He felt himself a social and popular person, and if with a smiling expression he could make somebody redden, he felt better still, because he was not only in a good temper but also one up on that person.

43

Jonathan did not redden but merely said, "My father taught you at the same age, but I think I shall have the better pupil."

"Wait till you try! It will be like teaching a caterpillar," said Sefton, grinning and taking up the reins. He touched his horse with his heels and went off at a canter.

᪣

Tolly felt he had been so successful as a detective that he spent the next day playing at being blind. He tried first in the house, feeling his way round the walls, surprised to find how difficult it was to tell that all four walls were not in a straight line but had right-angled corners. Indeed in this house few of the corners were right angles. The stone walls that were so imposing and certain to sight were gentle and curving to touch, almost warm, to be patted like living creatures. They bulged or sloped away, and their edges were blurred or broken off. The many recesses for windows or doors were deeper than the length of his arm, so that if he took his hand off the wall, he was quickly in empty space. And in space, even if it extends only just beyond one's reach, there is nothing to give a direction. When, after moving cautiously with outstretched hands, he met a piece of furniture, there was a pleasure in suddenly recognizing a brass handle or a row of bobbins along the rail of a chair. But they never seemed to be where he had left them. Or sometimes feeling out for the edge of a small table, his hands would meet a vase or

44

candle apparently floating in the air, which was startling, though it only meant that he was holding his hands six inches too high. The candle went flying, but fortunately not the precious glass candlestick. He soon found he was quite exhausted, so he took off the blindfold and went off into the garden with Orlando. After some crazy romping he felt better, and then he remembered that blind people had dogs to lead them, so he put Orlando on the lead and put his foot on it while he bandaged his eyes again. Off went Orlando straining like a cart horse. There was grass under his feet, then gravel, then grass again and Tolly very soon had an unreasoning terror of walking over the edge of the earth. Although he dragged back on the lead, it seemed to him that they went like the wind. He had no idea which way he was facing—every stumble left him more uncertain. Where was the wall, where the river or the moat? In a panic he let Orlando go and pulled off his blindfold. He was still on the lawn, facing back to where he had started from—the only direction he had not expected. The world whizzed round him into position again. He flopped into his great-grandmother's garden chair that was there in the sun and lay back to recover his self-confidence.

"Now I'll lie here and listen to what Susan heard," he thought, and at once realized how much wind there was, and how big, telltale, and friendly. It bumped into and passed round sheds; it crossed the gravel, bowling protesting dead leaves before it. It made a different sound in each tree, in some like the sea, in others like fretted tissue

paper. How it whirled the yew branches about! Tolly
could imagine the clouds moving like ships under full sail,
but Susan would know nothing about clouds or sky, and
never could. But surely somehow she would feel the *size*
of the wind? She could hear it approach from far away
and the immense hubbub of its passing. The birds were
trying to sing, because it was March, but the song was
interrupted, jerked out of their throats as they were tossed
off the branches by the wind and flew with an extra flutter
that reminded Tolly of rowing in rough water. He heard
the branches of two trees that leaned against each other
squeaking and groaning like an overloaded cart. He heard
the church clock strike one, and Boggis slipped past on his
bicycle almost as quietly as an owl. The sound was so
slight he opened his eyes to see if he had guessed right.
He heard a strange bird's whistle and Orlando barking

back. What kind of bird was that? It didn't sound like an English bird at all. He jumped out of the chair and went to find out. It seemed to come from the big beech tree. Sure enough, Orlando was standing up with his paws on the trunk barking to the sky each time he heard the whistle.

Tolly made a careful note of the distance between himself and the tree. I *will* walk there without looking, he decided, and set off with his eyes screwed shut. He walked and walked, stretching out his hands to feel the first beech twigs at the extreme end of the branches. But there was only empty air. He walked farther, as far as it could possibly be—but still only emptiness all round him. And there ought to be ivy underfoot, but there wasn't. Why was it all empty? Had everything disappeared? He opened his eyes and found he had hardly moved from where he started. His many steps had been timorous two-inch shuffles instead of paces. It was silly to be so relieved to find the world was permanent. He joined Orlando under the tree and peered carefully for a bird, but without finding one. Then something fell and hit the ground sharply beside Orlando, who snapped it up and gamboled off, pretending to shake it dead. Tolly ran after him and pried open his mouth to get it. It was a large fir cone. Out of a beech tree? Tolly, the detective, thought that needed explaining. A squirrel perhaps. A monkey? Well, this was the second time Orlando had behaved queerly under this tree. It must be explored.

At lunch he discussed his morning's experiments with Mrs. Oldknow.

"It's very tiring not having eyes," he said. "You have to

47

think everything out. But do you know what I have discovered? After my eyes, the most useful things I've got are my feet."

"Not your hands?"

"Well, you can't feel anything unless it's there to feel. There's an awful lot of emptiness. But there's always something under your feet. And they're quite intelligent."

"Did you think they were only what's inside your boots?"

Tolly laughed. "I suppose I knew, but I never thought about how much they enjoy the ground."

"Babies' feet enjoy everything hugely."

"So do dogs'."

"So do cats'—more than any. What fun to draw your claws in and out and walk so paddily."

48

"Do you think horses enjoy their feet? Though of course they haven't got any," said Tolly rather sadly, not liking horses to be without anything.

"Oh, immensely, in a leggy sort of way."

Tolly was curling and stretching his toes and generally enjoying the feel of his feet under the table.

"I'm going to climb the beech tree this afternoon," he said.

"Mind the rotten branches. There are so few you forget there might be any."

She spoke as though she climbed the tree frequently herself.

Tolly, who had got into the habit of thinking of her as Granny Partridge, grinned as he imagined her flying up with a whir. She met his grin with her wrinkly smile that still had something boyish about it, something rather like his own, as if she could read his thoughts.

"All your family have good heads for height," she added as she helped him to apple pie, putting his mind to rest on that score.

When they had washed up together, Mrs. Oldknow, with a guilty smile, brought out the patchwork.

"I'm like the other old lady," she said. "I do enjoy it. And it's too windy for me outside today."

"Would you like the fox fur muff? It might make you think things."

"No, thank you. I don't like thoughts creeping up my legs."

"I don't think Susan's grandmother can have been at all

49

like you. Supposing I had been blind! I am sure you would have been just as nice to me as you are now."

"Thank you for those kind words! I hope I should. But that grandmother was a leftover from severer times, a North country woman. And in any case, in those days children were very strictly, even cruelly, brought up, and punishment was thought extremely good for them. The grandmother was Susan's most forbidding teacher. Sefton was spoiled, but she was determined Susan should not be. Every Sunday afternoon she taught her the catechism and the creed, and a great deal about hell fire and all the most terrifying stories such as Abraham and Isaac, or Elisha and the bears. She told her how good it was to be patient and miserable and how ready God was to be terribly angry. She piled it on specially for Susan because she had to be more patient and more miserable than most people, so it was better to learn it young. She received Susan in the dining room—which was this room—and that was the only part of the instruction that Susan liked, because of the smell of the wood fire and the fruit and the flowers, and the different sounds on this side of the house. Beyond the tinkling of the prisms on the candelabra and the muffled ticking of the big gilt clock under its glass dome, there were all the sounds of the yew trees and the garden and lambs and sheep in the neighboring field. From the nursery she heard the weir, the river, and the boats, but from this side she heard the road with carriages and carts and riding horses passing along it. It sounded long, free, and exciting. She could recognize the parson's horse going past—a slow old thing—and the apothecary's that trotted flinging out one foot. At this time of the year she could hear the frogs in the moat. She tried to imagine from their voices what frogs could be like, and thought of them as little men, perhaps the size of her doll, dressed in wet window-cleaning leather, which was her idea of slimy but quite harmless. Their concert amused her privately as she listened to her grandmother croaking on about the vanities of this world. It seemed to her that the frogs in their ridiculous way sounded so contented that they must be enjoying the vanities, whatever those were, as much as the wood pigeons, whose cooing reminded her of her mother's chuckle.

"The grandmother did not enjoy the lessons any more than Susan, who could *not* be taught to stop fidgeting, so in order to be able to endure doing her duty by the child, she allowed herself the luxury of sewing her patchwork on a Sunday. This was how it came about that Susan, mad with having to sit still and listen, discovered on the ground between them the box full of paper and the box full of bits of stuff, and began to fold one over the other."

" 'Show me, Granny, how you do it,' she begged. And because sewing is generally hated by little girls and often given them for a punishment, the grandmother gave her a threaded needle and let her try. The one thing she never did was to prick herself. After a while she learned to tack quite well. It was something to do, and, besides, it was her own idea. It was fun too to recognize the stuffs— her mother's saffron muslin, the dimity curtains from the nursery, her own Sunday dress with raised spots, her father's ribbed waistcoat.

"Off you go now, Tolly. I *must* be getting old. I think everybody has time for talking. But of course they haven't."

❦

The difficulty in climbing the beech tree was to start. The bole was vast and smooth and the first branches came out of it too high to reach. They were, however, long and drooping and swept the ground far out from the center. Tolly straddled one of these at waist height. It was springy on its own account and also it was swinging in the wind, like a narrow boat pitching and tossing, but there was not far to fall and he swarmed up it to the trunk. Here the branch he stood on was as firm as a beam, but he still could not reach the one above. He came down again to study the tree from below. Orlando, who was keenly interested, sat down and looked at him as if wondering why he didn't get on with it. Tolly went off and got a rope from Boggis. It was harder to swarm up the branch carrying the rope, which caught on everything as much and as often as if it had a determination of its own. Arrived at the trunk, he leaned against it for balance while he tossed the rope up. He then realized how much harder it would be to grip a thin rope than the one in the gym at school, which was as thick as his arm, so he doubled the rope accurately and tossed the ends over the upper bough. Of course it hung wide, and the retrieving of it was the nastiest part of the business. He then braided the strands and made a fat knot at the bottom. With this he climbed up easily, and after that another branch was always within reach. As the tree was not in leaf, he had not the comfort of a green curtain hiding the ground from his eyes. On the contrary, he could see every branch off which he would bounce on his way down if he fell. However, up he went till, about halfway as he guessed, he stopped to rest on a comfortable branch with a fork where he could lean with one foot against the bole. He looked at the sky and the network of tree above him. "It is like climbing the rigging of the *Woodpecker*," he thought. And there, right beside his foot, he saw cut in the smooth bark and greened with years of rain the letters S and J. "J for Jonathan? S for Susan doesn't make sense up here. S for Sefton I suppose." Tolly felt quite annoyed that Sefton had left his mark and began at once to climb higher. At the next possible resting place there were the annoying initials again, S and J. This was quite as high as Tolly felt he could go without being sick, but the initials challenged him and enraged him. "I'll go higher than King Fox," he thought as he grimly felt for the next heave up. As he swung on his stomach across a bough trying to get his legs up, he could look straight down the trunk, which almost tapered to the ground. A very little Orlando was at the bottom watching him. However, the climbing became easier as he went on, though the thin upper branches

repeated the pitching and tossing that he had had at the beginning. Right at the top there was a kind of natural crow's nest, almost a star of branches where one could sprawl and swing at ease, and between two of them, where at some time the bark had been injured, a pocket had grown in the trunk. Could this be where *that bird* nested? He was about to put his hand in when he noticed the initials again, but this time only J. It was some comfort that Jonathan had got higher than Sefton. He groped around in the hole and felt all manner of unexpected things. For a minute he was afraid that Jonathan had stolen the jewels. He wanted to find them, but he did not want Jonathan to have taken them. He brought out a handful very carefully in case a string were to break and all the stones disappear in the ivy underneath. But alas, when he

54

studied his fistful, it looked more like a magpie's hoard than jewels—a silver button, a pearl button, several cuff-links (none of which matched), a key, a spur (far too heavy for a magpie to carry, surely), several small cut-glass bottle stoppers. Bottle stoppers? There was one in the "magic" box among Susan's things. Somebody loved magic. Somebody loved bottle stoppers. No, not Jonathan.

Tolly lay there for a while rocked gently by the wind and delighted with his bird's-eye view of the house. The roof was very steep and wavy. At the point of each gable there was a stone knob on which the thrushes sat to sing. He had always thought they sat there to be high, but now he was higher than they, so perhaps they only went there to have all that empty space to themselves. He could just see into the top of the chimney. If he could only throw the spur into it, how surprised Mrs. Oldknow would be when it fell into the hearth beside which she was sitting sewing her patchwork!

Tolly put everything in his pockets and started to come down. When he reached the most difficult part, he prepared to swing down from a bough where he would have to hang by his hands, letting his arms be pulled like elastic while he felt for another branch with his toes. "Now," he said to himself, "let's see how much sense my feet have got." After that he was back at his rope and the rest was easy.

Orlando welcomed him down, and they scuffled together as Tolly lay on his back to enjoy the solid ground and look up to where he had been. When he rolled over to avoid Orlando's tongue, the spur in his pocket jabbed his thigh, and he got up and ran in to report his finds to Mrs. Oldknow. Before showing them, he went into the kitchen and polished them up. Then he set them out in a glittering row in front of her one by one.

"The cufflinks have got a monogram, an S with an O in the middle," he showed her. "And the spur has a running fox engraved on the plain part. Look, it's wearing a crown."

She put on her big tortoise-shell spectacles to look.

"King Fox! Boastful boy! What a commotion there was when he lost it! Yes, these are all Sefton's. Fancy hiding them up there, the monkey!"

"It couldn't have been a monkey. There were initials carved by the hole. J. Why should Jonathan play at being a magpie or a monkey? He was grown up. But there is a big bird in that tree. I've heard it twice. Only I can't see it. And Orlando is as interested as if it was really a monkey. Is there a monkey? Could it be a monkey imitating a bird?"

"Bravo! As a detective you are full of ideas and hot on the trail. I think you have deserved another chapter tonight."

"How do you know so much, Granny?" Tolly asked after they had had tea and washed up, and Mrs. Oldknow had brought out her patchwork.

"Telling it helps me to remember," she said, spreading out the quilt. "Dear me! What a hole in the Captain's shirt!

My nursemaid, you know, was dear simple Ivy Softly. All these stories were handed down in the Softly family and told me as a child. And sometimes like you, I learn something from *them*."

⊸ JACOB ⊱

In the winter of 1795, when England was at war with France, the frigate *Woodpecker* was part of a convoy sent to the West Indies, taking reinforcements to put down a Negro insurrection in the Windward Islands. Their destination was Barbados. They had a difficult voyage. Twice they were driven back by storms to the harbor they set out from and had to stay for repairs and better weather. All told, it was six months before they arrived. They found the port crowded and in great confusion. Another convoy taking merchant ships to Jamaica had run into a strong fleet of French ships, and in the battle the English ships were separated, some were sunk, some captured, and the rest battered and full of wounded were now in Barbados. Townsmen and children, both black and white, stood about to watch and exchange news and rumors, and point out the ships to each other. The air rang with the noise of hammers and rattle of chains and the shouts of shipwrights. Besides all this and the uproar caused by the arrival of Captain Oldknow's convoy of troops, there was a multitude of smaller ships berthed there, mostly slave traders, and the compounds near the docks were full of chained Negro slaves. Captain Oldknow was one of the many Englishmen who loathed the slave trade, but though it had been abolished recently on English soil, it was still allowed in the colonies. He was glad that in the Navy he had little contact with it, whereas the captain of a merchantman could not escape it, for slaves were the most profitable cargo. The most the Navy had to do was to protect the lives of all who sailed under the English flag whether black or white. As he strolled through the streets the next day, thankful that in spite of many perils yet another journey had been safely made, his thoughts turned as always to Susan, and he looked for something to take home to her as a fairing. His wife and Sefton were easier to find presents for, if more expensive. Lace and combs of tortoise shell and Indian gold work from the Spanish Americas, wonderful leathers, tobacco and snuff, walking sticks curiously carved or of smooth slender ebony—it was a question of choosing. But Susan? Boxes of strange woods beautifully made—she never had too many of those, but one must think of something different. He was in no hurry. He had a week or more before he was to sail home. He came presently to the slave market, where often the slaves for sale had been brought direct from West Africa and looked like wild, unhappy animals. But there were always some changing hands who had been in slavery for a long time already, who were herded into the market place obediently like farm horses, some with their children running free beside them. At this time there was an unusual number being sold, because on many of the West Indian islands the slaves had mutinied and wherever possible were siding with the French, under a promise of Liberty, Equality, and Fraternity. The ringleaders were being rounded up. All those suspected of an inclination to mutiny were being shipped to America.

The Captain paused against his will to watch, disgusted by the heartlessness of the traders and moved with ashamed pity for the slaves, for England still allowed slavery and he was English. His curiosity was caught by a small Negro boy with a look of brilliant if anxious intelligence. He was wearing nothing but a shirt. The first time the Captain saw him, he was standing close beside a sad slave, who, one would suppose from the casual way the boy leaned against him, was his father, in the batch due next but one to be marched on board. After the leading batch had been moved away, the Captain looked for the child and found he had slipped back and was again in the next batch but one, looking trustfully up at another possible father and asking questions. When the time came for this man to go, the boy was seen to be holding a horse as if under orders to do so, but when the owner appeared, he dropped behind a bale and, hidden from the rider but in full view of the Captain, noiselessly as a cat backed away on all fours. Apparently he was determined not to be shipped off and fairly confident that no particular overseer would look out for him if he could avoid attracting attention. In his brief public appearances he managed to seem to be exactly where he ought to be. In his disappearing acts he had eyes all round him and the quickest calculation and ever changing enterprise.

Seeing the Captain looking at him kindly, he disappeared for a time, to materialize later from behind a bollard, when he tugged gently at the Captain's coat and whispered urgently, "Captain, buy me?"

"Run along, boy," the Captain answered. "There are no slaves in my house."

"Captain, buy one slave?"

"No. Not even one slave." He smiled at the little head, oval like a grape and almost blue-black, until it was split by an engaging grin. Too late he realized that it was no smiling matter, and his heart smote him. He put on the grim expression that people wear when they are too sorry and walked away toward the main street with its avenue of palm trees and its shops with awnings against the sun. He stood looking at the objects displayed.

"I'll buy Susan a tortoise-shell fan. She can open and shut it and it will make a noise like a bird's wing. The very thing." But before he could go in to buy it, he felt that gentle tug again.

"Captain, buy just one very little slave?"

The eyes were big and liquid and desperate, but as they met the Captain's, that irresistible smile was put on again— not deceiving but courageous.

"I said NO." But the Captain went into a cookshop and came out with a sugar bun, which the boy was eating ravenously almost before it was in his hand. And as he began to eat, the tears began to roll, shining down his dark face.

"Who do you belong to?"

"No one. Old man dead in fighting. Bang! Bang! Mammy taken away. Jacob lost."

"Who did your father belong to?"

"Him dead too. Bang! Bang!"

At this salvo for his late owner, Jacob grinned again, and the tears gathered over the bulge of his cheeks and ran down into his teeth and the vanishing sugar bun.

The Captain was very tenderhearted toward children, but he argued with himself that a man could not take responsibility for all the unhappiness in the world. There were millions as helpless as this Negro child. Plenty of orphans at home in England needing help, whose fathers had been killed fighting in all these years of war. He shrugged. "I'll get a fan for Susan," he repeated to himself, turning away. No gentle plea followed him as he had feared. Perhaps Jacob knew that a shrug is something you can't plead with.

When Captain Oldknow came out again with his purchase, a trio of slave overseers came riding up the street with their long leather whips in their hands and their wide hats pulled down against the setting sun. The avenue of palms was silhouetted black against the sun, and the man riding on the far side coiled his whip carelessly round each tree trunk as he passed it, pulling the thong free with a rough noise over the fibrous bark.

Captain Oldknow, looking after them, noticed that one

of the trees on the near side had a slightly knobby outline. The dazzling orange light pouring round it was notched at a child's shoulder height. But the three riders went by it without looking back. As soon as they had passed, Jacob's body slid round the tree, and seeing the Captain still there, he gave him a confidential, independent grin. He bore him no grudge for refusing to protect him. Jacob was on his own again, one against the world.

Captain Oldknow walked on up the avenue. As he passed Jacob, he put out a hand and brushed his head in farewell. Jacob could hardly take his eyes off the dangers and chances of the world long enough to look up at him. The Captain stopped and took hold of the neck of Jacob's shirt.

"Come along, Jacob. I'll find out whom I ought to buy you from. You shall grow up free."

Jacob who had jumped like a startled cat when he felt himself caught, beamed with a kind of solemnity at these words, and without further comment began to walk beside his friend with a growing confidence and even a certain childish swagger. Every now and then he would glance upward to see if it was still true.

"Come into this shop with me," said the Captain. "You need some pantaloons. You can't go to England in a shirt."

Jacob stopped at the threshold and made what was evidently a vow of loyalty.

"Jacob very good boy. No steal. No tell lies. Fight all Captain's enemies. Bang! Bang!"

Captain Oldknow laughed and pushed the child in front of him, suddenly resuming all his authority.

"Get along in, you little scapegrace." And to himself he added, "What an unimaginative clod I am. A fan to open and shut indeed! We'll try something inexhaustible."

He had no sooner reached England with his return convoy than the *Woodpecker* was sent to relieve another ship in the blockade of Brest, so that he did not arrive at Green Knowe till the spring, after fifteen months away.

When he told his mother and Maria what he had brought for Susan, there was a great outcry. The grandmother said, "You have brought the son of a murdering mutineer and a black heathen, at that, to look after your helpless innocent! Who knows what pagan wickedness he may teach her? It's a most ungodly notion."

"I had him baptized by the chaplain, and we must teach him religion. Jacob and Susan can do lessons together. It will give her confidence, because already she will know a great deal that he doesn't."

"How do you know he won't steal?" Maria joined in. "Nothing will be safe. I shall be terrified for my jewels. And what will the neighbors say? The fashion for black pages is quite out. Nobody dreams of having one now that they can't be slaves."

Mrs. Softly threw up her hands and rocked madly in her rocking chair.

"A black boy! Whatever next. As like as not, he'll cut her blessed throat."

"Jacob is as faithful as you are. He won't let anything happen to Susan."

63

"She doesn't need anyone to look after her as long as I live. Nothing *ever* happens to her. I see to that."

Sefton only laughed and exchanged looks with his mother. It amused him to see his father attacked by three "petticoats."

"You're introducing a plaguy lot of commotion into the house, Father," he said, knowing that after the discipline of a ship nothing tried his father so much as women's outcry over which he had no control. His father frowned and stiffened.

"This is an experiment that I wish to be given a fair trial. I think Susan lacks both amusement and exercise, which Mrs. Softly cannot be expected to give her. I shall give Susan to Jacob as his own especial charge, to serve, to amuse, and to protect."

"Sounds like the marriage service," Maria whispered to Sefton.

"I shall give Jacob to Susan as her own lieutenant, to carry out her wishes. I wish the boy to be well treated. When I am not here, if Jacob should fall short of what I expect from him or get into bad company, you are to apply to my old friend Morley and he will decide what to do. And you, Sefton, are by no means to appropriate the boy for your own service. He is not under your orders."

"Really, my dear, you grow more eccentric every time we see you," said Maria.

The grandmother sniffed.

"It's not only eccentric. It is WICKED." She rapped on the floor with her cane.

Susan, now eight, dressed in her best for the great occasion, was brought down to welcome her father. Her skin was very pink and white from being so much indoors, and her excitement at his home-coming was that of a child unused to joy who has waited for it almost too long. On hearing his voice, she wrenched her hand from Nanny Softly's and ran recklessly in his direction. Jacob was watching in the background as she found her father and wound violent arms round his neck.

"That's better," the Captain said. "I thought you had grown too dignified and reserved when I first saw you." He took her on his knee and tipped her face up to examine it.

"You have grown thinner, lost your round baby cheeks, and your mother has put you into a very pretty grown-up dress. Too much of a young lady for eight years old. However, I have brought a present for a fashionable little madame. Feel in my pocket."

"Your breast pocket, Papa? There's only your wallet in there. Is it in that?"

"No. Not in that."

"Your tail pockets then? Stand up please, Papa." In the tail pocket Susan found a parcel and wriggled onto his knee again to open it.

"When did you learn to untie ribbons?"

"My doll has one. And Nanny Softly has taught me

65

how to tie it in a bow. But she won't let me tie my own because she says I crumple them. What can this be?" She felt the fan and began to spread it gently.

"Is it all right to do this? Am I breaking it? Oh, it's a fan."

"From a very, very hot island."

Susan fanned herself, but without screwing her eyes shut against the wind as seeing children do. She let the fan slip back to the closed position and fall open again. And it made a noise like a bird's wing.

"What is it made of, Papa?"

"Tortoise shell and Spanish silk."

Susan let it fall open and shut, and continued to do so while they were talking. Sometimes she fanned him, sometimes herself.

"How are the lessons going with Jonathan? Do you enjoy them?"

"Yes, Papa. He reads me lots and lots of stories."

"Which story do you like best?"

"*Robinson Crusoe*, Papa."

"Which part of *Robinson Crusoe* do you like best?"

"Where he finds Man Friday. Papa, what did you do on that very hot island?"

"I dined with the Governor, and I waited till the merchant ships had unloaded and loaded again with sugar and cotton. And I restocked my ship and I bought an opossum muff for my mother, a fan for you, and a mantilla for your mother, and an Indian saddle rug for Sefton."

"And then?"

"And then I bought another present for you."

"Another? Two?"

Captain Oldknow beckoned to Jacob, who all this time had watched wide-eyed, to come nearer. He came soundlessly and, obeying the signs made to him, knelt at their feet.

"What's that?" said Susan immediately. "What are you doing with your hand, Papa?"

"Give yours to me." He guided it to Jacob's head.

"Oh! It's alive!" Her shy hand flew off, but at a chuckle from Jacob came back again, and the other with it. With unusual confidence she passed them slowly over the firm roundnesses of his face, and then over his neck and shoulders to his thin childish ribs, where her startled palm met for the first time a heartbeat that was not her own.

The grandmother, unable to control herself any longer, gave one sharp rap on the floor with her stick.

Susan shrank back on her father's knee, clutching his coat.

"Who is it, Papa?"

Jacob answered for himself, in a voice whose smallest half-utterance Susan was never afterwards to mistake for any other.

"It's me, Missy."

"It's a monkey," said Sefton, making his sneer sound as if it might be good-natured teasing, so that his father could not do more than look sharply at him.

"What a tease you are, Sefton." Maria laughed with him. "It's a good thing some of us can laugh at this extraordinary scene."

"This is Jacob," said the Captain. "I have brought him to be a playmate for you."

"Is he blind, Papa?"

"No, my dear. He has eyes for two. That is what made me think he will lend them to you." He put Susan off his knee. "Go with him into the garden. It's his first day in England. The stage coach was so crowded he couldn't get near the window. Take him out into the sun."

"Just us two, Papa?"

"Just you two."

They went out together silently, hand in hand.

When they were alone, Susan said, "There is water all round the garden. It is called the moat. And there is a river that drowns people. Nanny only lets me walk on the paths, but Papa takes me this way on the grass. It is very exciting. There are animals that are trees."

They turned left beside St. Christopher, and Jacob shied like a horse and then stood still.

"Very big Juju man," he said.

"Not Juju, his name is St. Christopher, but I don't know him. He is too big to touch." Jacob was much impressed.

"Not good to touch Juju man."

They went on together along a little path among the trees. The water rats plopped into the moat and the moor hens hurried into the reeds or overhanging ivy.

Now and again Jacob said, "Tree put out arm here," and he ducked under it, and Susan, feeling his movement, ducked also. It was more fun than having things

68

moved out of her way, which made space so empty. Presently Jacob whispered, "More Juju. Antelope Tree."

"Why do you keep saying Juju? What does it mean?"

"You not know Juju? Witchdoctor make Juju, keep bad things away. Tree Antelope here, like Missy say."

"I expect it's the Green Deer. Take me to it, Jacob." Susan liked the Green Deer. It was better than the rocking horse because it was soft, and with the sun on its leafy coat, it was, if not exactly warm, at least alive. And it was springy, not rigid. She put her arms round its neck and stroked it from its ears to its stumpy tail, and it left a tangy smell of yew on her hands.

"Over there," she said, pointing not quite in the right direction, "there's the Green Squirrel. And the Green Hare."

"I see tree animal with big tail, bigger than body."

"That's the squirrel. And the tree bird with a big tail, bigger than its body, is the peacock."

"Is Tree Antelope Missy's own Juju? Missy make Juju? Blind missy make very strong Juju. Wild animal never hurt her. Walk up to lion, he go away. He not understand why Missy not frightened. He look angry, blind Missy not notice, so he frightened and go away. Elephant not hurt blind Missy. He feel with trunk, Missy feel with hands. Elephant understand. All animals know Missy very special. Serpent not sting. Crocodile not eat." It was turning into a triumphal chant, in which Susan soon joined, and because she was used to learning

69

things by heart, it turned into a rhyme almost without thinking.

> Tiger, he not claw,
> Lion, he not spring,
> Buffalo not gore,
> Serpent not sting,
> Elephant will understand,
> Horse come to hand.

Somehow a tune grew with the words, and with Susan holding onto Jacob's shirt, the two of them marched round the garden chanting at the top of their voices.

Captain Oldknow watched them from the window and called his wife.

"Maria, my dear, come and look. This is the best thing I have seen for years. Who could tell, seeing her now, that Susan was not like any other child?"

Maria amiably kissed the top of his head as he leaned back in the chair.

"How inexplicable all you men are! There's Susan with muddy patches on her new dress and the frill torn at the hem, caroling with a little black savage, and you think it's the loveliest thing you've seen for years! Oh dear, isn't life amusing! However, so long as you are pleased! It doesn't very much matter what Susan does. It isn't as though she went anywhere. But I've always taken a pride in dressing her beautifully. Do me justice in that."

"You turn her into a doll, my dear. All curls and

laces and ribbons. My mother will say that I am a Jacobin, but I do believe in liberty, especially for children. Let her rip. There's time enough for her to simper later."

"Bah! You only say it to vex me. But I'm in a good humor. I won't be vexed. Now you are at home you can take me to Lady Overman's ball."

"I am afraid I shall have to leave you again for a short time unless you come with me. I must go to London for a week or so."

"Oh, what can you possibly imagine I could want more? Sefton can take my place at Lady Overman's. Bachelors are always welcome."

"I must tell Sefton to see the tailor and get two suits of clothes made for Jacob. I couldn't fit him out in Barbados. No woolen cloth there. On board, the sailors wrapped him up against the wind. I couldn't see much of him, but I gave him a quarter of an hour of my time every day to keep an eye on him, and an hour on Sundays, and I had excellent reports from the ship's officers."

"Shall we put him in page's livery?"

"No. Just inconspicuous good clothes."

Meanwhile, Jacob, after exploring the rambling garden, was sitting on the grass with Susan, telling her his own racy version of his successful escape from the slave traders. ("Captain buy me, and pay for me," he said with proper pride.) Then followed his voyage back in the *Woodpecker*, and from the Juju figurehead on the prow to the

71

groaning of the timbers, the whistle of the wind in the rigging, the perpetual slopping and slapping of water, the harsh flapping of sails, loud as gun shot, when the ship altered course, Susan received it all at first hand with minute guns and sailors' calls and sailors' curses thrown in plentifully, which neither of them understood but both enjoyed, for they were not only funny in themselves but belonged to the real grown-up world. Jacob mimicked too the way the sailors spoke to the Captain, alert, abrupt, and disciplined, and the jokes they made among themselves afterward ("Old Sharp-Nose wasn't taken in. Not likely. That nose would do for a compass needle."). This gave Susan a new view of her father's standing. She ran her finger thoughtfully down her own nose, and then down Jacob's.

"Your nose is like the cat's, Jacob."

"No, Missy. Nose like lion."

The rolling of the ocean swell was done for her. With her hands on Jacob's shoulders she could imitate it with cries of "Here she comes! Up she goes!" and hands clasped over the stomach for the sinking sensation.

"Ship sail many, many years," Jacob ended—he had not much sense of time but a very good idea of a story—"across great ocean and see no land at all, till one day ships come up from everywhere all going to same place, sea full, no room for any more, all shouting and singing, and flags flying, and many, many gulls come, all gulls in world come and settle on ships like they their own. Then Captain bring Jacob in rattle-bang coach all across big

72

island to this little island in middle, very full of ghosts, and much Juju, and Missy."

&⋅⋛⋚⋅&

"What a long story," said Tolly. "It's quite hard to come back to *now*. I wish I'd been here with Jacob."

"Aren't you? What about that un-English bird in the tree?"

"Oh . . . So J is for Jacob."

"When did you hear the bird first?"

"When I was sitting pretending to be Susan, trying to hear what blind people hear."

"Well, you did."

"Orlando did too. And he is always wagging at people who aren't there."

"I told you he had made friends."

"Do you think he sees Jacob when I don't?"

"Dogs aren't so dependent on seeing. They just know." Tolly kicked his heels in displeasure.

"Doesn't it make you feel stupid," he said.

The next day, just as Tolly was going out to climb the other trees in the garden, particularly the yew that in the winter had been the snowhouse, a sudden March shower came on, with thin drops like driven needles, and every tree was dripping. The beech tree looked the wettest because of its fishskin bark. He would have to amuse himself indoors.

"I'm going to find something else," he announced. "There's sure to be a corner where something's stuffed away. Isn't it a good thing that people can't bear throwing things out? I wonder where I haven't looked. Which was Sefton's room?"

"You must remember the house used to be much bigger. Sefton's room was in the part that has gone."

"Was the kitchen the same as now?"

"The present kitchen was the butler's pantry."

"That horrid Caxton dressed like a wasp? I shall look there."

The kitchen was lined with cupboards, and it looked very promising. Nobody, thought Tolly (who knew nothing about spring-cleaning), looks on top of tall cupboards. And it was true that nobody had looked for a very long time. He drew a picture of Caxton in the dust. At the back, against the wall where it had been pushed every time anyone had dusted, was a roll of cobwebby drawer paper. In the middle of the roll was a bottle of gin. Tolly came down the stepladder sneezing and dirty. Next he tried the most difficult corners of the top shelves where there were stacks of odd pieces of china that no longer matched anything else. Among them was a charming mug with *Susan* painted on it in gold, which he brought carefully down with him. That was nice, anyway. The very bottom shelves of the lowest cupboards were dark, damp, and inaccessible. Tolly lay on his stomach and shone his flashlight on piles of baking tins, rows and rows of empty jam jars, bottles of turpentine and metholated spirit and

linseed oil. He opened with great difficulty rusty tin boxes
that contained only soda crystals or black lead. It was all
terribly sensible, except perhaps the gin. That could be
Caxton's, and it would show that he did hide things. Under
the sink there were buckets. It was a damp, awkward place
with the S-shaped trap for the sink pipe getting in the way
of his head. It must have been a place where the cold pipe
often froze, because where it went through the wall it
had been neatly boxed. Not nailed—screwed. *Nobody*
would look for jewels there! Tolly fetched a screwdriver
and got to work. Inside, the pipe was wrapped round with
mildewed and moth-eaten cloth, tied all along with a spiral
of thick string. It was bulky, and when Tolly pinched it,
there were hard lumps inside. Breathless at the thought of
rubies as big as nuts, he cut the string and unwrapped the
cloth. A crumpled coat and trousers, and his rubies were
tarnished brass buttons! After all that! And unscrewing
old screws is very hard work. Then in the cleaner folds of
the cloth he recognized the green and red materials in
the patchwork. A green coat and red trousers, in thick
cotton—like school sheets. Not too displeased with his
finds, he carried them off to show Mrs. Oldknow.

"Here's some more of your patchwork," he said. "Will
that do for tonight's story?"

"It will do very well. It comes just where we left off."

"You didn't finish yesterday. You never told me about
the tree, except that the bird was Jacob."

"I will tonight."

"I've got an idea."

"I've learned to expect that."

"Do you remember how I used to put out sugar for Feste? I'm going to put something for Susan. It's stopped raining."

He ran out into the garden, now brilliant with sudden sun, and for just a few minutes before the drops vanished they hung like diamonds on every twig. Then, as the sun drew up the moisture, the air was scented, so that Tolly could hardly bear to let his breath out. It seemed a waste. He was looking for scented flowers, but the strongest and most exciting smell of all was the earth itself. He picked violets and viburnum and tiny sweetbrier leaves and made them into a tight bunch. This he put in Susan's mug and took it upstairs. He went in cautiously, looking toward the child's chair, innocently empty. And now a difficulty arose. Where was he to put it so that she would find it? He moved a small table near the chair and put the flowers on it.

"Ooh! What a lovely smell. It is like Mama's perfume."

Susan was sitting on the window seat threading beads. Her hair was hazel-gold against the light, and she looked very serene.

"What shoes are you wearing, Jacob? They sound different."

"It's not Jacob."

"Oh, it's you again! Do bring the flowers here. If I get up, all the beads will spill."

"I can't," said Tolly. "I—" But he was alone.

"Why couldn't you? You could, you know," Mrs. Oldknow said later. "Susan can't see you. She's easier to approach than most people."

"That's what makes me feel mean. Being a ghost to someone who doesn't know you are."

"Tut! You lost your courage. Well now, about the green and red suit."

◆§ MONKEY CLOTHES §◆

Captain Oldknow and Maria had gone to London for a fortnight. Sefton had stayed behind because it was the point-to-point season, and because when his parents were both away, he could do exactly as he chose, for he took no notice of his grandmother.

Susan was having her morning lessons with Jonathan, who had promised her something new. He could not reconcile himself to the fact that she could not read. He felt that he was not doing his duty or teaching her at all unless she learned her letters. So he had spent hours of careful and exact work in the evenings at home carving the alphabet onto a large board. He produced this for the first time on the day that Jacob, round-eyed with curiosity, joined them. Jacob thought reading was just more Juju. How else could black marks be spoken words, words that were alive and powerful and made things happen? Jonathan had a fit of despair about teaching Susan the whole alphabet and decided the one really essential thing for her when she grew up was to be able to sign her own name. So he took her finger and put it in the groove for S. When you think of it in shapes, S U S A N is an easy word. Jacob hung over the table breathless with concentration. This was Susan's Juju mark.

"S is for Snake." ("Serpent not Sting," he thought.)

"Quite right, Jacob! Very good. S stands for Snake." When the letters had been learned, the difficulty was for Susan to write them. Jonathan could never imagine a problem until he ran up against it. Susan with a piece of chalk put her U lying on its side and A upside down. But he couldn't show her what she had done. Jacob's eyes were going from Jonathan's puzzled face to Susan's blind fingers. He was nothing if not resourceful. The evening

78

before he had been in the kitchen watching with envy the pricking and patterning of pastry. The cook had not let him try. "Don't you put your black fingers in my dough," she had said, picking up the rolling pin.

"Missy write snakes in dough," he suggested hopefully.

One of Jonathan's virtues was that he could take a good idea when it was offered to him. He rang the bell for Caxton, but at the same moment there was a knock on the door and Caxton stood there with a tape measure.

"Mr. Sefton sent me to measure Jacob for a suit. I'm to go along this morning to the tailor. A rare menagerie you've got here, Mr. Jonathan."

Jacob's face was a study in pride as he stood to be measured.

"He thinks he's the admiral," Caxton sneered to Jonathan.

"When you have finished, Caxton, please ask Cook to send me up a large tin tray with some pastry dough."

"Anything to oblige the gentry."

The dough was sent, and when it had been rolled out flat with a round ebony ruler, Susan wrote into it with a slate pencil, and made her mark, and could feel it.

Meanwhile, Jacob was absorbed in rolling thin dough snakes between his palms and bending them into S's.

"Missy make snakes in dough, roll up and eat. Very strong Juju."

"The dough was a good idea, Jacob." Jonathan gave him the credit due to him. "Now Miss Susan will learn as quickly as you, if not more quickly."

79

Jacob had soon learned the names of the letters, but still thought A was for hut and N for 'Nocerus horn.

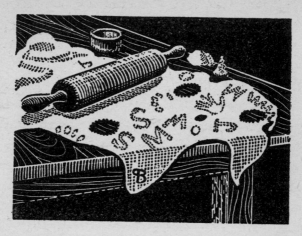

Every afternoon when it was fine they went together into the garden. The grandmother, peeping out of the window one day to see what they were up to, was horrified to see Jacob pressing Susan's head down to the ground by the back of her neck and heaving up her feet—not to murder her but to teach her to turn somersaults. Susan had always been taught to walk as carefully as if it were the most difficult thing in life not to fall, in a world beset with water, fire, staircases, high windows, open doors, and pits. And now there she was, outside, where anyone could see her, her dress fallen round her armpits and her white cotton tights bottom upward to the sky. The old lady knocked furiously on the window frame with the knob of her cane, making signs of consternation that Susan could not see and Jacob could see no reason for.

He only looked behind him as if there might be a lion in the bamboo. Mrs. Softly was sent panting out to them.

"Miss Susan! Making such an exhibition of yourself! Oh, my goodness! I wouldn't have believed it. You indecent little hussy. And you, Jacob, you bad wicked boy. I'll tell the Captain about you."

"I'm being a wheel," said Susan and did it again.

"Wheel go round and round," Jacob yelled in encouragement. "Horse pull very hard." And he bowled himself along the lawn. Susan came up laughing with her mobcap over one eye.

Nanny Softly was painfully out of breath with shaking her featherbed figure in such a long run. While she gasped for enough air to speak again, she reflected that, though shocking, the game was only childlike, no real harm in it. So she only grumbled, "I never thought to see you behaving like a gypsy as knows no manners. Pull your skirt down. Now stop it and sit down quiet."

On this particular afternoon the extraordinary tinny but festive music of a hurdy-gurdy struck up at the front of the house. Hurdy-gurdies were fairly common in the towns but rare in the country. They were played by melancholy Italians, usually accompanied by a monkey who attracted the children and took round the hat for pennies. The monkeys were dressed in green coats and red trousers, from the back of which their unhappy tails dangled, no longer used for a gay swing from tree to tree, for they were chained.

"Take Miss Susan to hear the music, Jacob," said Nan-

81

ny, glad to sit still. "If there's a monkey, don't let her get too close."

There was a monkey, crouching on the painted hurdy-gurdy, looking as cross as two sticks. Its coat skirts trailed round its heels, and it scratched its armpit dejectedly.

"Is there a monkey, Jacob?"

"Slave monkey, very sad. Missy want monkey?"

Probably because of Jacob's gentle fearlessness, the monkey did not bite when he took hold of it but only jibbered and rolled its sharp close-set eyes in sockets as wrinkled as the Sahara. Jacob settled it comfortably on his arm. The hurdy-gurdy man till then had done nothing but gaze at the upper windows and turn the handle. It was always from the upper windows, from maids or nurseries, that the pennies fell.

Jacob felt in his pocket and handed Susan an apple.

"You give it."

"Toopenss to feed monnky," said the enterprising Italian, still gazing skyward.

Susan held out the apple, which vanished from her fingers, after which there were open-mouthed eating noises.

She felt robbed. A vanishing apple, but as far as she was concerned, no monkey.

Jacob held out his hand for hers.

"Monkey not bite. Missy scratch under him chin, feel big lump in cheek where him hide apple. Feet like hands. Long tail hang down."

At the touch of her hand the tail came to life and

82

curled firmly round her wrist, then with a squawk and a rattle of chain the monkey leaped away.

"Nanny!" shouted Susan louder than she knew she could, and she bounced up and down with satisfaction. "We want tuppence."

A window opened and Betsy, the housemaid, threw down a handful of pennies with a pert, "The missus says that's enough, thank you." The tune stopped in the middle of a note, the pennies were gathered up in frantic haste as if they might be asked for back, and the hurdy-gurdy man trundled away down the drive. He was passed by a boy bringing a parcel from the tailor.

"Here's your new suit," said the housemaid, giving the parcel to Jacob. "If you're getting tidy for supper, you'd better put it on."

Jacob went up to his room (he slept on a pallet in the little closet that opens out of your room, Tolly) to put on the clothes that were going to make him like everybody else. It was a solemn moment for him. But the suit was not at all what he had expected. It was not like English boys' clothes. However, he was sure the Captain would give him what was right. So he put on his suit—it had a bright green coat and scarlet trousers like a soldier—and went downstairs again.

In the hall Sefton, just coming in from shooting, was handing his gun to Caxton. When they saw Jacob, they roared with laughter and slapped their knees and cried "Oh, ah!" and held their sides. Sefton called for the housemaid Betsy, who admired him, to come and look. And she put

83

her hand over half her face and rolled her eyes and said, "Oh, Mr. Sefton, what have you done! Oh, what a dreadful wag you are. Oh dear, he looks just like the monkey that was here this afternoon." Then she put her apron up to her eyes and rocked with laughter.

"Was it here this afternoon? That's too good to be true. I got the idea from one in St. Neots. Thought ours ought to keep up with the fashions. Musn't lag behind the times." Sefton could hardly speak for laughing.

Mrs. Softly came to see what the noise was about, and Sefton said, "Come quickly, Nanny; I'm dying of a stitch in my side. Oh!"

Mrs. Softly looked severe for a moment, then shook her head at him.

"Well, I don't know! Mr. Sefton, will you ever learn to be serious? I'll be bound this is one of your pranks. If Caxton measured for that, I don't congratulate him. Why the sleeves and trousers are six inches too short. Turn round, Jacob, let me— Oh, my gracious! There's even a slit up the back for his tail to come through. Come along with me, boy, till I sew it up. Oh! Mr. Sefton!"

She dragged Jacob away, while laughter broke loose again, the unbridled, contented laughter that follows a cruel joke.

"Where's Missy?" Jacob asked as they went upstairs.

"I put her to bed. She's tired like a dead thing."

"Me go to bed too, tired like dead thing."

"You stay here till I sew up the back of your pantaloons.

84

Mr. Sefton must have his joke we know, but *that's* not Christian."

"Me no wear monkey clothes any more."

"You wear what you're given. They've been ordered and paid for, and money's not for throwing away. You leave them here tonight, and I'll lengthen the sleeves and the legs."

"Jacob no wear monkey clothes."

Susan's voice came from behind her drawn bed curtains.

"I want to say good night to Jacob."

"Stop talking and go to sleep."

"If I can't say good night to Jacob, I won't go to sleep. I won't go to sleep EVER, all night. And I'll be terribly thirsty every minute and you will have no peace all night."

"What kind of talk is this!" Such defiance was quite new.

"I'm terribly thirsty now. I want a drink. Get me a drink please, Nanny. And I want Jacob."

"I'm here, Missy."

"Jacob, feel my cheek."

He parted the bed curtains and there she was in a frilly nightdress, one cheek stuffed up quite out of shape.

"What you got in there, Missy?"

"Nuts," she said when she had with difficulty let them out again onto her palm. "Was it as big as the monkey's cheek? Jacob, wasn't the monkey exciting?"

"Plenty monkeys in black man's land."

"I like monkeys. But I don't like Sefton."

"If Mr. Sefton want monkey, he get plenty monkey business. You see, Miss Susan."

"Jacob, are frogs like monkeys?"

"Miss Susan want frog? Jacob bring one tomorrow."

"Good night, Jacob."

When Mrs. Softly came back with a drink of milk, Susan was already asleep.

("Did Jacob really have to wear the monkey clothes?" Tolly was anxious.

"No. It was only Sefton's joke. He told the tailor his father had brought home a rare monkey from South America and wanted clothes for it urgently because it would die in the cold March winds. So something was run together in a hurry, and the real clothes came later. They were ordinary, decent, and just like anybody else's, because Sefton left that to the tailor. He wasn't interested enough to choose them himself. The grandmother was angry about the monkey clothes, not because Jacob had been made fun of, nor because she thought, like Nanny Softly, that every human being has a dignity that must be respected, but simply because Sefton's behavior had been "idle" and he had laughed with the housemaid. So she gave the monkey clothes to Caxton "to give to the poor," and she used the left-over bits that the tailor sent with it for the patchwork.

"You haven't told me anything about the tree yet."

"Oh dear, I shall never get to the tree. You find things so quickly I can't keep up with you.")

Well, the next morning Jacob got up very early, as he often did, and went off into the garden on some business of his own. There were also possibilities he wanted to explore in the house before Sefton came down. Later Jacob had his breakfast in the kitchen and then joined Susan for lessons. They were both impatient for more letters. Jacob insisted on shutting his eyes while he did them. They mastered the new letters J A C O B and wrote them in dough. While they were doing this, a disturbance broke out in the house. Sefton's voice was heard clamoring that a silver button was missing off his riding coat and he couldn't go to the races till it was found.

"Caxton, you cleaned the buttons this morning. Why didn't you tell me one was missing?"

"They were all there when I cleaned them, Mr. Sefton."

"Well, be quick and find it. I can't go out with buttons missing like the hurdy-gurdy man." At the word hurdy-gurdy, Sefton's guilty conscience supplied a possible answer. He stormed into the schoolroom and seized Jacob by the shoulder. "Where's my silver button, you black monkey?" But the button had passed from Jacob's hand into Susan's when the noise first began. Jacob was solemnly innocent, protesting while his pockets were searched and rolling his eyes to heaven. The commotion continued all over the house, coming and going, stairs being swept, rugs shaken, Betsy all devotion, Sefton furious, and Caxton in a cold rage. Presently Susan asked, "What letter is for monkey, Jonathan?" and when the black finger and the pink finger met in the groove of the M and pushed each other,

87

the children laughed till they had to be called to order.

In the garden after lessons—it was lovely weather and about this time of year we're in now—Jacob left Susan throwing crumbs and listening to the birds while he went to a certain overturned plant pot. Then he came back.

"Missy want frog? Him very slippy, very cold. Jump further than horse. Must hold back leg tight like trap."

She held out her hands, and Jacob, holding it by the leg, laid the frog in them. Susan felt the cold, gentle clutch of the frog's hand round her finger and felt also that it had a rapid near-the-surface heart.

"Frog have eyes at corners of head, big like Indian corn." Susan felt and recognized the blink of a tiny wrinkled lid.

"Ai, he pull! Leg very strong."

"Let me." Susan held the leg, but when the frog pulled, her heart failed and she let it go for pity. She heard the slow, long hops sliding through the grass and, as she and Jacob followed it up, the final splash as it reached the moat.

"Frog home again with him wife."

"Now bring me a bird. A live one, not Sefton's horrid dead things." Sefton had once terrified her by throwing into her lap the mask and paws of a fox. "Bring me a fish, and a bumblebee, and a mouse and a rabbit and a horse and a bear and an elephant. Bring me something every day."

"Ai! Miss Susan want lot of very hard things."

"Bring me them."

"Yes, Miss Susan." Then after a pause, "You got silver button?"

"Here it is."

"Jacob put it in good place. No steal, only hide." He was gone a long time, while Susan sat still and the birds came nearer and nearer, their wings purring past her ears, moving her hair. She heard an unusual bird whistling very high up, and a dog barking. The frogs were croaking like people lazy in bed. Somewhere there was the rhythmic thud of Boggis digging. Close at hand there was a leaf twirling in the wind on its twig. It sounded to Susan like a candle in a draft. When Jacob came back to stand beside her, he absent-mindedly picked it off.

"You put the candle out, Jacob. Now you're in the dark."

"The candle, Missy?"

"Yes. You pinched the wick."

Jacob looked at his fingers.

"No. Missy. No candle. Leaf shaped like candleflame. Make the same noise."

"Where did you go, Jacob?"

"Up big tree, high like *Woodpecker's* crow's nest."

"What was that dog? It wasn't one of Sefton's."

"Little curly dog, come when African bird whistles. . . . Tomorrow I think Mr. Sefton have only one cuff link, untidy like hurdy-gurdy man."

Minor annoyances now beset Sefton every day. He seldom could find more than one of any pair, and as he was a dandy, there was plenty for Jacob to choose from—

embroidered slippers, lace cuffs, scent bottles, shoe buckles. As Susan's hands and wits were quick, nothing was ever found on Jacob, and nobody thought of searching Susan. Their partnership was so good that a glove or a glass stopper would vanish almost before Sefton's eyes.

"Where the devil did I put that thing?" would freeze Susan and Jacob into pictures of solemn, sympathetic innocence.

"What has Sefton lost now, Jacob?"

"Don't know, Miss Susan. He lost somefin'."

Jacob was jauntily obedient, and there was nothing against him. The fact that never more than one of a pair disappeared ruled out Caxton, who if he stole would steal effectively. In any case he knew so many of Sefton's secrets that he could always squeeze money out of him if he chose. The other solution that Sefton with some pleasure thought possible was that the devoted Betsy was collecting souvenirs of him to put under her pillow for sentimental reasons.

"This is Betsy's striped print dress I'm patching now. She wore a fichu round her shoulders and a mobcap. Pretty, she was. But I don't mind covering up her patch. I can still buy striped cotton, though it's not as nice."

Tolly sat listening to his great-grandmother's needle pricking in and out of the paper that her bits were sewn on, and the harsh sound of the thread pulled through it. His eyes wandered over the patterns within patterns in the folds of the quilt, and he heard the fire and the clock, and the blackbird in the beech tree, and Orlando galloping in dreams as he lay flat on his side on the carpet, and airplanes going overhead droning in unlimited space. All these sounds seemed held in a very old and wonderful silence.

Tolly pointed to a rose-colored patch with tiny white sprays on it.

"Susan was wearing that when she was threading her beads. I saw it."

That evening when Tolly went to bed at the top of the house, it was not yet dark. Through the dormer window on the west he could see the sunset fading out through red to purple. Through the opposite window looking east, the world was darkening so rapidly that Tolly realized he was actually *seeing* the earth turning away from the sun, instead of seeming to see the sun dropping in the west. It was a dizzy thought. He imagined the crow's nest on the *Woodpecker's* mast, swaying to east and west like a metronome, with the sun moving up and down to match it. He wondered how high in the rigging Jacob, who was his own age, had climbed. He went to the closet where Jacob had slept to re-examine it. It was quite small and had no window. His school trunk was put there in the holidays, and, except that he had a special personal feeling for everything in Green Knowe, he had not thought twice about the closet. He now lit his candle and went in, closing the door behind him. He set the candle on the trunk and sat down beside it. The walls were bare except for two clothes hooks. There was nothing at all to make a shadow but himself—that is, if it was really his. Could he do magic with it? he asked himself with a peculiar feeling at the top of his spine. He twiddled his fingers and the black fingers twiddled on the wall—of course. But all the same he did not like it. He went out, and then felt brave again, and took another candle, saying to himself that now there would be two boys, which was not as bad as not being sure if the shadow were his own or a black boy's of the same age, and if the fingers had really done exactly what he did, or had done it with a difference. He put the new candle at the opposite end. Now there was one boy but two shadows, and the shadows could meet and pass through one another, could add up to one and separate again to two.

"Jacob," said Tolly in a whisper, which sounded very loud in the closed closet.

There was no answer, but Tolly caught his breath because he imagined for a moment that something had pressed against him.

Mrs. Oldknow still came up every evening to say good night to him, for their mutual pleasure. She found him not yet in bed, but leaning out of the window in his pajamas, looking at the first cherry blossoms showing whitish in the half dark, and the evening star reflected in the river.

He put his arm round her partridge waist.

"There are a lot of things Susan couldn't see," he said.

"She could smell, you know."

Tolly took a great breath of the spring night.

"Do you think she could smell stars?"

"I nearly can myself tonight. She could certainly smell the kind of thing that stars belong to and happen in. Sometimes you make things smaller by giving them a name to themselves, like 'star.' Imagine Susan taking a breath of it and just thinking *all that*."

Tolly took a lungful of star and cherry blossom and fresh-water river and yew and sleeping violets, and then leaped into bed.

"I've been looking for Jacob in his closet, but I only scared myself. I hope I don't have bad dreams."

"Why ever should you?"

"I don't like being touched by things I can't see."

"That's one of the disadvantages of having eyes. They make people afraid when they can't see. Everything that touched Susan was something she couldn't see. But far from being afraid, she wanted to catch everything in the act of being real. She even put her finger in the candle flame to see what being burned was like. Now go to sleep. Tomorrow is another day."

Tolly went to sleep, but for some reason he woke very early, when it was just beginning to get light, too soon for any bird but the thrush to be awake. He looked out of the window and saw the garden dim and far below, with wisps of mist caught in the bushes. When the thrush was silent, there was not a sound in the world. The garden

93

was waiting to be brought to life. He dressed and slipped quietly downstairs and out, feeling inclined in the half-light to keep near cover, to move carefully and look and listen like a wild animal. He didn't know if he was play-acting or not, the dawn was so hushed and hushing. The bamboo hedge and willow thickets seemed to be the places of most attraction. Bamboo is jungle-like, beautiful, light and swaying (though not swaying at all now, but still as in a trance). No one can see what is hiding in it, and any bird that is startled there makes a loud rattle of canes and stiff leaves as it breaks out. Tolly crept along, watching the ground because a fallen cane in the rough bumpy grass could easily trip him up. He heard a startling, rushing noise close behind him, and two swans passed low over-head, the sound of their flight, once they had gone by, continuing far up the river, and in the water underneath them their reflections flew upside down. After that the world began to tick, faint tuts and chucks, and little flutters and cracklings, as the birds woke up, talked in their sleep, stretched their wings, scratched their ears, and shifted their positions. And all the insects did the same. Even the leaves had a look of waking up, lifting them-selves a little toward the sky as it got bluer. The thrush was singing quietly now from the knob on the point of the gable, and a robin close to Tolly's ear was just trying under his breath to see if he was in voice, when a moor hen shot out from under the bamboo calling in a panic to her chicks to come away from danger. Several bobbin-sized babies ran after her, but there was one brown fluffy

thing by Tolly's feet trying hard to obey its mother, yet
finding every twig an obstacle too hard for it. As it was
trying first to duck under and then to climb over a matted
stem of wild rose lying in its path, a slim black arm came
out of the bamboo. Careful fingers closed over the chick
and withdrew it, squeaking murder into the bushes. Then
a voice said consolingly, "You not get hurt. You go little
while under my plant pot for Missy."

Tolly dropped onto his knees and parted the canes to
look in. He could see nobody, but shortly afterward Orlando was standing behind him, wagging doubtfully with
the guilty looks of a dog who has been out with the
wrong master.

The sun was now up, the birds all busy or singing to
congratulate themselves. Near the moat the cheeping of
moor hen chicks went on and on. Tolly felt very hungry

and went indoors. Inside the house it was neither yesterday nor today but somewhere lost in between. In the living room the patchwork curtains were drawn across the three big windows. They let in a colored gloom like stained glass, darkened by the surrounding yews. He had never seen the room like this before. Nothing could be more mysterious—a room for Rumpelstiltskin to rage in, for a stepmother's mirror, or a sword that spoke. In the evening the many colors of the hangings were festive in the firelight, but now, drawn against the day, they seemed to be shielding old secrets. The smell of the house was heavy and strange. Orlando's ears cocked this way and that and his nose twitched. Into the hearth a gray shaft of light came down from the chimney, such as creeps into caves from a sloping crack in the roof. It was so different from the brooding, over-beautiful twilight enclosed by the curtains as to look like something coldly evil. Tolly was seized with a violent wish never to meet Caxton. He took newspaper and an armful of willow logs and made a bonfire on the wide hearth. It roared up the chimney with a draft that pulled all yesterday's air up with it and the room was today again, filled with delicious willow-wood scent. He lay on the hearthrug to watch the fire while he munched biscuits.

It was still far too early for Mrs. Oldknow to get up, so he went out again, to climb the biggest yew tree, the one that had been the snow house at Christmas, where he had first met Toby. The woodpecker was hammering

in it when he got there, but flew away with a flash of
scarlet. It was an easy tree to climb, the branches
coming out at regular intervals in a spiral round the trunk.
At the top he lolled very happily, warming himself in the
sun, feeling as much part of the garden as the birds, the
mice, and the moles. The sun seemed hotter up there than
on the ground. The scent of the whole yew tree beneath
him was drawn into the upper air, along with the willow
smoke from the chimney. Tolly sang his favorite song of
the moment (which happened to be "A-sailing down
along the coast of High Barbary"), and the upper air took
that away too. He understood now why thrushes have to
sing so loud. The thrush came and perched on its gable
knob a stone's throw away and entered into determined
competition.

Mrs. Oldknow came to the living-room door.

"What a serenade! Come down and have some bacon."

Tolly found plenty to amuse him in the days that followed. He was allowed to take a pair of hair-cutting scissors
and trim up the Green Deer, the Squirrel, the Peacock,
and the rest, which he did quite well. He ran errands for
Mrs. Oldknow on her bicycle, and she never minded how
dirty he got in the garden with Orlando. Mrs. Oldknow
took him to visit a neighbor who made a hobby of model
ships and helped him to repair the *Woodpecker*. Tolly
spent many happy hours learning about the sails and the
tackle. But the finish of every day was the same and always

looked forward to by Tolly. The patchwork was brought out, and the baskets full of bits, and the story began.

⊷§ THE CHIMNEY §⊷

Poor old featherbed Mrs. Softly, who got so out of breath when she ran into the garden to stop Susan turning unladylike somersaults, had a bad heart and was ordered to bed. Susan went politely every morning and evening to ask how she was and to show if Betsy was keeping her clean and tell her not to worry. Susan's bed was moved into her grandmother's room, which she hated because it was stuffy and smelled of camphor and medicines and old bed hangings. If you have ever smelled woolen tassel trimming, you will know what I mean. It was cluttered with screens, footstools, workboxes, small tables, and thick fur rugs, which made it difficult for Susan to move about.

However, there were advantages to Nanny Softly's illness. It was a time of sudden and unimagined liberty. Betsy, who had to carry trays up to the sickroom and Susan's meals to the nursery, and was supposed to feed Susan too, decided that this was too much extra work for one person and gave Jacob and Susan their meals together so that Jacob could feed her. This was Susan's chance, and if at first she ate with her fingers, Jacob was not the one to stop her. Before long she promoted herself to a knife and fork, and if the knife skidded and the meat flew across the room, Jacob simply retrieved it and put it back on her plate. They had an amusing, messy time together, and Susan learned by leaps and bounds.

Jacob also was learning many things. He admired and envied with his whole heart Jonathan's power of reading aloud to Susan. He wanted to be able to give her this great pleasure himself. His own wonderful powers of imagination and storytelling he counted as nothing beside the printed word. Consequently, he learned quickly and his English improved. It was he who tumbled to the idea of teaching Susan simple arithmetic. It happened naturally while they were playing a garden game of keeping shop, with bay leaves, mint, and hawthorn "bread and butter" sold by the sprig and with hazel nuts for coins. He continued to bring her everything that struck his fancy—fir cones, dandelion clocks, fossils, birds' eggs, butterflies that beat softly against her arched hands, hyacinths like ornate steeples carved in wax with a smell she was never to forget, tulip buds, and woolly stalked polyanthus. Besides all this, there was her list of requests. The first bird, as you know, was only a chick, but when Jacob put tiny, tender rhubarb-pink worms on her palm, she soon had the robins and tits. He brought her a wildly flapping fish, which she was sorry she had ever asked for. You will not be surprised to hear that they soon had a mouse, nor that they spent a lot of time together in the stables. Jacob played hide-and-seek with her in the garden as her father had done in the study till she ran freely on her own, guided as much by scent as by foothold and hearing. He let her lie on the riverbank and plunge her arms in to feel the pull of the current and to hear the gurgling.

One day he was busy braiding long strands of ivy stalk, at which she took her turn, to make something like the *Woodpecker's* rigging for her. Sefton and a neighbor were shooting in the river meadows beyond the house. They came back with an equal number of rabbits and a partridge each. Sefton, however, claimed to have winged a mallard.

"No, sir, he fly very strong over this way," said Jacob, pointing, with some satisfaction showing in his voice.

"I saw him fall, somewhere here."

"No, sir, no duck fall here."

"When I say I saw it fall, I saw it fall. I'm not blind."

"I heard it go over," said Susan.

"I suppose you can distinguish a mallard's flight from a teal's, Miss Know-All."

Sefton looked round about. "It could have fallen on the roof." He winked at his friend. "Or down the big chimney. Let's send Jacob up to look for it." He grinned in his reckless good-natured way, and his friend grinned back with no disguise of pleasantness.

"It would never do to have a flue blocked by a stinking bird."

"Better than having it blocked by a stinking black boy if he stuck in it."

"He won't stick in it. What are boys for?"

"I stay look after Miss Susan. Captain say I not your servant. I not go up chimney."

"You do go up chimney. Sweeps' boys go, so why not you? You're the right color already. Why, it won't even show. You won't have to wash afterwards, if it's washing you don't like."

They seized him as though it were a great joke and frog-marched him into the house, Sefton laughing and showing his splendid teeth, and his friend sniggering.

Caxton was in the room laying out the mail and newspapers that he had just fetched from the post.

"Can you imagine any reason, Caxton, why a black boy shouldn't go up a chimney to fetch a beautiful mallard that is lodged there?"

"None at all, Mr. Sefton. Very suitable and right."

"Off with his coat and trousers! Send him up in his drawers."

Sefton and Caxton took Jacob by a leg each and hoisted him up until he could find finger and foothold in the uneven bricks. He hung there straddled across the opening, which was almost too wide for his stride, though it narrowed higher up.

"Hurry up, or I'll light some newspaper to give you an up-current."

Jacob nearly fell twice, amid delighted chuckles of "Look out! Here he comes!" But he kicked off his shoes (one caught Caxton on the nose), and digging his agile toes into the cracks, he finally got going, and then it was easier. He pulled himself up till he reached a ledge where he could rest out of sight from below.

Sefton and his friend stepped out of the hearth, shaking

the fallen soot from their hair and cuffs, while Caxton came forward with a brush to clean their shoulders.

"Active little monkey," he said. "He'd make a good sweep's boy."

"That's what he ought to be. Not playing around with my sister. If he was a year or two older, I'd put him in the way of the press gang."

Susan had followed them in, and now they heard her voice behind them.

"Where's Jacob?"

"He's up the chimney, my love. Can't you hear him?"

Susan heard the muffled dragging noises relayed by the chimney from the unvisited hollows that go through the center of a house. She followed the edge of the table round till she knew by the smell of his clothes and hair and the nearness of his breathing that she had reached her brother.

"Sefton?" She didn't want to make any mistake.

"What can I do for you? You can't go hand in hand up the chimney, you know."

Susan kicked his shins repeatedly with all her might, but he was wearing gaiters and hardly felt it. He laughed as though this was the best yet. Each kick made him laugh.

"Hey! You passionate little madame! Take her to one of the women, Caxton, and bring us the sherry."

"I won't go with Caxton. I'll go by myself." Susan made for the door, holding her hands in front of her in case the door was open and its edge jutting out into the room.

"She'll be a nuisance when she starts creeping round by

102

herself," she heard Sefton say. "I shall laugh if that blacka-moor comes out in Mrs. Softly's fireplace. We shall hear her screaming from here."

Meanwhile, Jacob on his ledge up the chimney, though his eyes were smarting and the soot on his lips was nasty beyond anything, was considering with interest the unex-pected features of the shaft he was in. It was nowhere abso-lutely dark. A ghostly grayness traveled down it. He knew that every room had a fireplace but had never even won-dered about the course of the flues. He had just presumed they all went straight up. The one he was in—though when he had looked up from the bottom toward the dis-tant square of sky, it appeared to go straight—did in fact travel sideways at regular intervals. These sloping pas-sages would be easier to climb, and as the flue narrowed all the way, the worst was over. The mysterious cavity about him looked positively inviting; the soot felt to his fingers like moss. He would go up till he could stick his head out of the top and surprise Susan in the garden. He would call out, "Miss Susan! I stick out of chimney high up in sky." And she would hear how high and defiant it was. He proceeded on his adventure without another thought for Sefton.

As he had supposed, it got easier as well as lighter toward the top. Where bricks were broken or projecting, he found oddments dropped by birds, straw, sticks and moss, snail shells, dead mice, broken eggs. While he was changing his foothold with his cheek pressed to the chim-ney side, he saw lodged in the soot near his eye something

103

that gleamed faintly. When he had made sure of his balance, he looked for this again, feeling with a spare hand over the bricks. It was not till he had shifted his body and a ray of light from the top fell on the soot that he was able to pick it out. A child's ring with one small pearl, probably dropped by a jackdaw. He sucked it, and rubbed it on his hip, and it shone like a moon no bigger than a robin's eye. He put it in his cheek for safekeeping. He was now almost up—just one more sideways bit and then the top. He gave a vigorous downkick into what he thought was a heap of soot and stubbed his toe on iron. A small square iron door, such as sweeps use, was let into the wall at this point. Jacob shoved; the door opened outwards and swung to rest against the outside wall with a clang, while its rusted catch that had broken off fell down the chimney hitting first one side and then the other. Susan sitting sadly beside her grandmother, who had fallen asleep over a book, heard these hollow noises from no known place with terror for Jacob. He, however, had scrambled through and found himself in a seemingly vast space under the roofing tiles. At his back was the big stack, and leaning against that, he could stand upright. To left and right were other smaller stacks, which came up in pairs to meet each other and formed arches under the roof tree. From there the tiles sloped down to floor level, and the whole dusty, cobwebby area was lit by an occasional piece of glass set in instead of a tile. There were no floor boards, but here and there a loose plank had been laid across the joists to keep workmen from putting their feet through the ceilings. Jacob was ignorant about the construction of houses. As a slave in Barbados he had lived in a shack, and this was the first house he had ever been in. He picked up a short length of plank for no reason except that it was loose, and again for no reason balanced it on end and leaned on it as on a crutch. It immediately pierced the ceiling, and Jacob fell sprawling over a joist. Luckily he did not swallow the ring, which he now put on his finger. He hauled the plank back, dislodging a lot of plaster, and lay peering through to see what was underneath.

From his unauthorized viewpoint the room he looked into had quite a different appearance from the ordinary rooms that one lives in. For one thing, it was the wrong way up. He looked down onto the floor, where the whole pattern of the carpet showed up like wallpaper, on which was set furniture that seemed to have no legs, or very short ones. To Jacob, lying above in the dark, the light sliding in through windows in the room below did not look like the streaming sunlight that all men share, but like the light of a peep show, artificial and dramatic. If anyone were to come in and walk across the floor, he or she would look frighteningly unreal. It was a luxurious room with a great soft bed hung with curtains. A man's room, because there were jack boots standing by the wall. What if it should be the Captain's room, the Captain's writing table and papers, that were now so deplorably covered with plaster and rubbish? But over a chair back hung Sefton's chestnut riding coat, its silver buttons shining.

Jacob heaved a sigh of relief and satisfaction, and getting to his feet, he deliberately made another hole larger than the first. The plaster showered down, covering the coat, and for a little while heavier grit trickled down the broken slats onto the carpet and pattered into the boots. When this pleasure was ended, Jacob, rubbing his hands on his seat with satisfaction, noticed that his pants had been torn in his scramble. With a smile growing wider and wider he ripped off as much of the material as would come away, and then carefully draped it over the end of the slats where they stuck down into the room. He hoped it would look as if he had fallen through up to his armpits and in struggling back had left the seat of his pants behind. It was his flag of defiance and contempt.

He then proceeded to explore, stepping carefully from joist to joist. Each chimney had an iron door at this level. Jacob tried to guess where the flues came from. In the old part of the house it was easy, in the new more difficult, especially as the new building was at right angles. After wandering around he came back to the big chimney, and close beside it he noticed a trap door let in between two joists. He heaved it up—and looked down into his own closet. With a whoop of joy he dropped onto his bed.

Meanwhile, Sefton and his friend were drinking sherry and throwing dice. Every time a trickle of rubble and soot rattled into the hearth they snorted with amusement, now and again getting up to see how far he had climbed.

"Going up like a lizard."

"It will be a lot harder coming down. Better not let him break his neck."

"He'll climb out at the top."

"How will you get him down then?"

"Oh, he'll shin down a drainpipe. Same as a coconut tree to him."

However, Jacob was now washed and changed and had slipped downstairs and out into the bushes to watch what was going on in the room. As he made his way through the bamboos, he had a piece of luck. He came across a speckled hen lying dead, probably dropped there by a startled fox who would come back for it later. Its neck was broken and a few feathers gone, but otherwise it looked freshly killed. Jacob put it under his jacket and made his way back unseen into the house and up to his closet. From there he climbed back to the iron door through which he had escaped from the chimney. His voice traveled down the flue as if through a megaphone.

"Mr. Sefton! Mr. Sefton! I got your bird. Shot clean through neck." The hen was launched, and Jacob shut the iron door and disappeared.

"Well I'm blasted!" said Sefton, half believing his own lie had come true.

The bird, with wings falling open, slithered and bounced in a cloud of soot and fell onto the hearth.

When Sefton saw what he held in his hand, he went scarlet, and it was his friend who laughed, hiccupping like a jackass.

"Never heard of a gentleman shooting hens before."

107

"Don't be an ass. Hens don't fly."

"How else did it get up there? Evidently they do fly when they see you out with a gun."

Sefton pushed over the card table.

"I'll wring that brat's neck one of these days."

His friend only laughed the more.

"Why did you send him up to get it if you didn't want it?"

Caxton, coming in as if to clean up the hearth before dinner but really to see what the noise was about, considered the now sooty and ruffled hen.

"Shall I give that to Cook with the rest of the bag, sir?"

"I suppose you mean that for insolence."

"Not at all, sir. But as you wish, sir. I really came to tell you, if I may, that unfortunately the ceiling is down in your bedroom, sir, the black boy not being in any way trained to the job. I have told the women to make your bed in the spare room. I hope that is what you would wish, sir."

Caxton made a mock stately exit with the dangling hen. That at least made Sefton laugh.

"He looks a fool anyway," he said, regaining his temper.

❦

Tolly's days were very happy. He fished in the river or looked for nests. He taught Orlando at the word "lie" to crouch where he was until Tolly, hiding in the bamboo or up a tree or in his own attic, should call him. He shot with a homemade bow and arrows and taught Orlando to retrieve the arrows. He sang at the top of his voice from pure pleasure in the sun and the wind, and when it wasn't "High Barbary," it was "Rio Grande." All the trees became like known staircases to him, with nests on the first, second, or third story. He tried to feed the sitting hen chaffinch with rhubarb-pink worms, but she sat obstinately unmoving in the hope that he would decide she wasn't real. He was losing his patience with her closed beak when chaffie himself arrived, and taking the worm from Tolly, offered it to his lady, who then accepted it. Of course when the young were hatched, they would take anything from anybody. He began to feel that he knew every bush and hollow of the garden—knew it with his nose and lungs, with his ears, with his feet and his palms that handled all the boughs as he climbed, even with the inside of his knees as he swarmed, and with his back and stomach as he lay on the grass. It was very much his own, and the weather was hazy, balmy, and trancelike. He continued to go out very early in the morning because then he could hear neither cars nor airplanes nor farm machinery nor factory sirens, and the heron might be standing on the edge of the moat looking like one of the pterodactyl family.

One evening he was looking for a lost arrow in the shrubbery, from which last holidays Green Noah, a yew tree cut into the shape of Noah, had been dramatically uprooted. The surrounding bushes showed thin patches where Green Noah had smothered them. It was a broken untidy corner that had not yet had time to grow together again. He squirmed about in the undergrowth, looking upward because often it is easier to see an arrow in silhouette against the sky where it cuts across the pattern of the twigs. He leaned on his hand and felt under it the firm support of an overturned plant pot. How would a plant pot get here where no one had done any gardening for so long? Suppose it had lain there ever since the shrub that first grew in it was planted out? Suppose it was Jacob's plant pot for keeping frogs and chicks under? Tolly lifted it up carefully, disappointed to find nothing in it but a worm that crawled away. He backed out again through the clutching berberis onto the lawn. Orlando was there, standing obediently with an arrow in his mouth.

Tolly took it from him, surprised to find that it was not his own. His were tipped with the metal ends of pencils and the feathers stuck on with seccotine. This was much more skillful, tipped with a sliver of slate in a cleft, bound with thread, and the feathers were set in a cleft too. It was also longer than his. It looked quite a dangerous weapon. He fitted it in his bow and drew as far as he possibly could, aiming at a tree trunk across the moat. The bow pinged, and he heard the arrow strike the tree and saw it quivering there, but when he had run the whole way round to the other side, he could not find it again, though he and Orlando searched for a long time. What Orlando did find was a rolled-up hedgehog, and this by way of experiment Tolly took in his handkerchief and put under the plant pot. The sunset was fading. He could see the light from the living-room windows where Mrs. Oldknow had lit the candles. The garden was not quite so much his own after sunset. He had not realized how dark it had become until he found his eyes could not follow Orlando, who was merely a shadow that came and went. The bamboo rustled and a frog croaked at long regular intervals as if repeating a warning. It was hard to remember that it was only a frog when the mist was rising and making shapes like things and a hush was closing in. He looked up at St. Christopher as he neared the house, but he could only just make out where he stood wrapped about with ivy and shadows. To one side of the statue and about level with its stone thighs, the house windows shone apricot. As Tolly turned toward the door, something metallic clinked against a pebble under his foot. He brought out his flashlight to look, thinking it might be the key, or his great-grandmother's flower scissors. It was an old jack-knife with a bone handle, the closed blade clogged with mud and rust, looking as if it had come to light when the gravel was hoed. He put it in his pocket.

"You're late tonight, my dear."

"Why do birds have to talk so much when they are going to bed? I wonder what they say."

" 'Nudge up,' I expect, just like children. You can pull the curtains now, please. I left them for you."

Tolly pulled the quilted curtains and brought out the

patchwork that was being mended and the baskets of
bits, and they settled down.

"Cut some more pieces of paper for me please, Tolly.
I have used them all up."

He lifted the corner of the quilt and shifted the folds,
checking up the patterns he knew already.

"There's Susan's curtains and her dress and her other
dress, and her mother's yellow dress, and the Captain's
shirt, and Sefton's riding coat, and his dressing gown, and
Boggis's shirt, and Caxton's apron, and the grandmother's
Sunday dress and everyday dress, and the monkey clothes,
and Betsy's print. Let's have something new. Tell me a
tale about—this." He brought his finger down on a piece
like strawberries, crimson with yellow pips.

"Ah, that!"

◄§ JUJU §►

After the ceiling in Sefton's room had been replastered,
he decided he would have it redecorated in a more up-to-
date way. He wrote to his mother, asking her to bring
him some of the fashionable striped material from London.
Meanwhile, he told Betsy she could have the old curtains—which were of the stuff you just chose—to give
to her mother. Now there was enough of the strawberry
material to make dresses for all Betsy's sisters and curtains
for her mother's cottage parlor as well, so when Jacob

asked with his most alluring smile if he could have just one little piece "for somefin'," she let him have it.

Jacob had been secretly busy in one of his garden hide-outs where he had collected a strange assortment of materials. Among other things he had obtained the skin of a poaching cat that had got itself caught in one of Boggis's rabbit snares. Needless to say, Jacob was there before Boggis. He had been watching the snares for some time and had already removed a rabbit. The cat—it was a fawn Persian—was pure luck. Out of the rabbit skin and a butter keg he had made a drum.

One afternoon there was a perfect opportunity to practice part of his plan. The grandmother was at church (it was Lent), Sefton was at a cockfight, old Mrs. Softly was still in her room and likely to stay there, and the rest were busy spring-cleaning. Betsy was glad enough to leave Susan with Jacob. She had no professional ideas about how clean a child should be in order to reflect glory on the one who looked after it. She thought clean once a day for a visit to Nanny was enough.

As soon as they were in the garden, Susan said, "What have you got for me today, Jacob?"

"Ai, Missy! Come and see." They went together to the hidden flowerpot and found it bumping about. Thin squeals came from inside it.

"When I come this morning with baby cuckoo, plant pot jump and squeak like now. Inside, small porcupine. I not ever put him there. Missy feel—all sharp thorns." The plant pot was lifted off.

"Oh! Jacob! Whatever is it? It's round like a spikey ball."

"Him baby porcupine. Roll up tight in ball so dog can't bite. Him put there by spirit of drowned sailor. Missy know that? Spirit of drowned sailor boy in garden—him climb trees like masts and sing sailor songs like on Captain's ship. Him fell off top royal spar in great storm and drown. Follow Captain and Jacob here."

"I have heard somebody singing, but I thought it was you."

"No, Missy. Drowned sailor boy. Big stone Juju man bring drowned boy on shoulder. Now we make big Juju and him go away, not hurt Missy. Listen."

Jacob began to tap the drum very softly. Susan was enchanted.

"What's that? What are you doing?"

"Missy beat drum—like this." He taught her the rhythm and soon the garden was waving and rustling to a sound never heard there before. But inside the house there was so much flapping of dusters and beating of chair seats, and outside so much beating of carpets, that nobody noticed. All afternoon they practiced drumming, and first Jacob stamped a dance, knees bent and posterior raised, and then Susan tried. Her dancing was very curious as she could not copy what she had never seen and had to invent it out of her own body. Jacob watched with approval, drumming for dear life.

"Ai, Missy! You make good witch woman. Tomorrow we do big Juju."

"How do you know it's a drowned sailor boy, Jacob? How do you know it isn't a real boy?"

"Him not there, Missy. Him sing sailor songs high in treetops and I see him not there."

"Can you see people *not* being there? If I heard him, I should know he *was* there."

"Missy not like other people. Missy very special."

(Tolly was looking at Mrs. Oldknow with eyes in which triumph and disbelief were so equal that only laughter could emerge.

"This story is all about me!"

"You don't say so!" she replied mockingly. "Well, to continue.")

The next morning a letter came from the Captain to say that he and his wife would be home in a few days. The message was brought by Betsy to the schoolroom where Susan was writing the whole alphabet in dough and Jacob on a slate. They each envied the other. Susan liked the cool feel of slate under her finger and the smell of slate pencil dust and the dragging noise of the writing. Jacob longed for beautiful podgy dough. Whenever possible their heads approached and they did a bit for each other. Susan found a little pearl ring in her dough that nobody could ever account for. It fitted her finger perfectly, and not even the grandmother could make her give it up.

Jonathan found it hard to be as strict with Jacob as he thought he ought to be, though Susan by her father's

116

orders was to be coaxed, not disciplined. He found Jacob
endlessly funny with his adventurous eyes and quicksilver
associations. It seemed too that Susan learned most easily
what came to her through him. Whenever their fingertips
met, or even their elbows, there was an exchange of
thought. To both of them, the Captain was the most
wonderful person living.

"Him come soon."

"Not 'him,' Jacob, 'him' is accusative. He comes, or he
is coming."

"Him bring Miss Susan little man out of his pocket like
Gulliver."

The spring cleaning was quickened to a frenzy to be
ready for the owners' return. As soon as lessons were over,
the children were packed out of the way to do as they
wished. Susan's desire was the drum.

"Today we make Juju," Jacob announced.

From his special hiding place he brought out his sur-
prises, his early morning work. He had taken a small
sack, and into its loose weave he had threaded the stalks
of silver willow leaves, carefully, in overlapping rows
to look like fish scales. This was to go over his head. But
first he had woven (remembering the basketmaking he had
seen on the plantation) a sharp osier beak. It was yellow,
open like a sea gull crying, and out of it lolled a tongue
of strawberry material! He contrived to fasten the beak on
his forehead with a strap. Over this he wore the sack
with a hole for the beak to come through and for him

117

to see out. For decorative eyes, he had filched for the occasion two of the round brass horse ornaments from the coach house and had fastened them on the sack. They were the more horrifying for being equally suitable for fish or sea bird. Jacob was too young when his parents were captured in Africa to have seen real tribal magic, but he had heard about it in fireside stories, and he quite understood that a Juju is many-sided, that it must be both magnificent and grotesque, both superhuman and less than human, in this case fish, bird of prey, man and beast, ghost and play-actor. So his fish-bird had a crest of cock's tail feathers (acquired simply by seizing and holding tight till the cock got away without them). These flopped like hair around the brassy eyes. For good measure he wore the lion-colored catskin, head downward in place of a tail, so that when he danced the cat sprang.

The beak, tongue, feathers, and fish scales, but not the eyes, were intelligible to Susan, but whether they conveyed awe I cannot say.

Jacob explained to her that they must lay presents for the drowned sailor boy in front of St. Christopher (big stone Juju man), and there she would drum and he would dance and the spirit would take the presents and go away.

"What presents shall we give him?"

"What sailor boy need."

Jacob produced a toy hammock woven by himself out of garden twine, a hymn book given him by the ship's chaplain, a canoe carved out of a small piece of wood, a homemade harpoon, and his own most treasured jackknife given him by an amiable sailor. This last terrible sacrifice he thought necessary to make the performance real.

Susan could think of nothing of hers that a sailor boy could want. "Give Missy's hair to make him ghost wife."

He cut off a hazel curl and wrapped it in the hammock. These gifts were laid on a pile of sticks and set on fire.

Susan couldn't wait any longer to begin drumming, and soon the ritual was in full swing, bare feet stamping, hands clapping, the basketwork beak turning to left and right, the catskin leaping and clawing behind. The bitter smoke of burnt paper and hair rose to St. Christopher's stone nostrils and Jacob's voice was raised in weird prayers or threats in his own language.

Most unfortunately the grandmother had not gone to church this time but had taken a stroll to escape from the unrest of spring cleaning and was now coming back through the garden. The tap of her approaching stick was not heard.

Her horror knew no bounds. She was as fierce and relentless as any witch doctor, clapping her hands and calling for Betsy, for Boggis, for Sefton, threatening with her cane and shrieking like a sea gull.

"Oh! You wicked, blasphemous, obscene heathen! You savage! The altars of Baal in our own garden! The shame of it, the bestiality! Susan, down on your knees, girl! The everlasting punishment—Boggis put that fire out—Sefton catch that boy. He ought to be flogged."

She drove her heel through the precious drum.
"Oh *NO!*" cried Susan and had her ears boxed.
Oddly enough Sefton, though he had no morals himself beyond a certain physical courage, was as shocked
as his grandmother by Jacob's drama. He caught the
fleeing Juju priest, who was hampered by his headdress,
and was dragging him back when Jonathan arrived, having
heard the grandmother's shrieks from the road. He saw
with astonishment the sack scaly with leaves and the fear-
fulness of the brass eyes and willow beak, though now
knocked rather to one side. The imagination and ingenuity
of the costume he admired frankly.

Sefton, his face quite changed with the unusual sensation of being shocked, handed Jacob over.

"Take the beastly little thing away and give him a real hiding. It's your job not mine. He's your pupil. I hope you are proud of him. Perhaps now my father will be convinced that blacks should be left at home."

The grandmother took Susan in and caned her hands hard for drumming on the idolatrous instrument, and made her sit and listen while she read out of the Old Testament about the altars of Baal and the terrible punishment of the wicked.

Jonathan took Jacob up to the schoolroom where he first listened to the whole story, which seemed to him nothing worse than lively imagination and make-believe. He did not for a moment believe that the drowned sailor boy was real to Jacob. He explained that St. Christopher was a Christian figure not suitable for Juju offerings even in play.

"And now for the beating. Be sure you yell loud enough for Mr. Sefton to hear, or you may get another from him." He raised his cane, and Jacob's eyes widened with apprehension, but Jonathan brought it down on the seat of a chair, thwack.

"Ah, you stiff-necked little sinner! You want it harder, do you?"

At the second thwack dust rose high from the cushion. Jacob yelled. After that they had a splendid whipping, and Jacob screamed for mercy enough to convince anybody.

121

"Now don't forget you can't sit down," said Jonathan at the end. "And I'll keep these things to show the Captain when he comes back."

"Will Captain be angry? Will he send me away from Missy?"

"I don't know. But not if I can help it."

Jacob left the room with a most doleful face, holding his hands over his seat. He was not allowed to see Susan again that day, but his acting of not being able to sit down to table was so convincing that Betsy's heart was softened and she gave him a special supper and a lollipop to take to bed with him. Susan had only bread and water.

⋘⧜⧛⋙

The mail came while Tolly and his great-grandmother were having breakfast, and as she read it, she tut-tutted and clucked and finally said she had to go to Greatchurch to visit a friend who was ill. That meant Tolly would be alone all day. He walked with her to the bus and then came home by himself. It was all very well to know so much about people who used to live at Green Knowe and to find nearly every day something they had left behind, but Tolly longed for somebody to be there now. Particularly Jacob. The plant pot seemed the most likely point of contact. Tolly had only once found anything under it, and that was a slow worm that could have got there by itself. He put under it a beautiful green and blue lizard and a piece of stone on top of the pot so that it could not escape. He hoped it would be well received. Susan liked things with hands.

This dense thicket, if only it were not so difficult to move about in, might hide many things. In the middle of the brambles, hawthorn, laurel, and berberis, there was a vigorous growth of traveler's-joy, which for want of something to climb up had piled up over itself in a dense roll of stringlike stems, now tufted all over with new leaflets like miniature shuttlecocks. It looked the very place for nests. Tolly cut some brambles away to make a possible entrance and went in under the branches on his stomach and elbows. A great deal of wriggling was necessary before his face came up against the lower coils of the creeper. He shut one eye and pressed the other against the matted stalks, hoping to meet the fixed stare of a sitting bird pretending not to be there. What he did see, suddenly close to him as things are when you look with one eye, was stone. An old wall, made of the same stone as the house. More wriggling brought him to an opening in it, made difficult of entrance by loose stones lying about that bruised his hips and knees. It was the remains of a round building, perhaps a watchtower, or a watchtower first and a summerhouse afterwards, but now only low broken walls and a jumble of stone. The roof had long since gone, but before it fell away the traveler's-joy had taken over and now provided a hammock-shaped ceiling under which Tolly could stand upright. This he felt sure must be where Jacob had made and kept his Juju clothes and other treasures, and no doubt in those days, even if ruined, it would have been easier to get to. Tolly looked round him with a beating heart. The walls were strongly built, thick, made for some serious purpose long ago. The one fragment that was still high enough showed a window slit of stone, through which a hairy trunk of ivy climbed out like a monstrous caterpillar. The roof of traveler's-joy was thick enough to keep out rain but let in enough light to see by—a straw-colored twilight. It was the most perfect hide-out a boy could imagine. For a time he just sat there thinking of Fair Rosamund and all the bowers and woodland houses in ballads, and Sir Tristram when he was mad in the forest. And he forgot all about Jacob and Susan. Then he realized it was too quiet, as if someone was keeping very still. And Orlando was cocking his head as if he had heard something that he was not easy about. Tolly, who had at first thought it quite perfect, a dream, now felt a wish to break the spell by altering it to suit his own use. He began to roll away from the middle of the floor as many of the stones as he could loosen and range them as seats round the walls, but many were knotted together by ivy and firmly bedded in roots. He made his way out again to fetch tools.

It was a Saturday. Boggis had mowed the lawns, and the garden smelled deliciously of hay and sweetbrier hedges. Now he had gone, and except for the countless birds in the garden, the airplanes overhead, and the occasional jump of a fish in the river nearby Tolly had the place to himself. He lay on the grass to eat his sandwich lunch. He was willing to give Orlando a fair share, but Orlando made him feel that every mouthful he ate himself was the meanest thing anyone ever did, so it went very quickly. Then Tolly leaped up and took the garden shears to cut an easy tunnel through the undergrowth for his coming and going, and a pick and spade to clear the floor, and went back to his bower.

It was hard work. Orlando, however, was keener every minute. He was a born digger. As the work went on, he concentrated his blowing and scratching under one particular stone. Tolly came to help him, heaving till the stone moved and there was a sound of gravel pouring down a hole. He twisted the stone sideways and saw Orlando disappear into the ground. At first he thought he had fallen into a well, but there was no splash and he could hear Orlando scrabbling not very far below. He brought out his pocket flashlight and shone it down the hole. It showed a flight of stone steps, with Orlando standing at the top, out of reach of his arm. From floor level to the step was a drop of about three feet, the opening covered with a rotting wooden lid. Tolly went to work with fresh energy until he had cleared a space the width of the stairs. The floor of the tower room was flagged, he found, and the wooden trap door had been hidden under a stone very much thinner than the rest to make it easier to lift. It was also more easily broken, so that at some time a falling block had smashed it. Tolly had only to clear away the bits and lift the trap door, which just gave room for a person to lower himself into the tunnel. He joined Orlando and peered down into the descending stairway

125

now dimly lit from above. It had a sharp mouldy smell. The walls were slimy to touch and the steps slimy to tread on. Orlando was suddenly anxious not to go first, insisting on following down on Tolly's heels, upsetting his balance and threatening to send them both sliding down out of control. At the foot of the steps the passage was high enough for Tolly to have walked easily, had it been in good repair. The walls bulged as if about to fall in at any moment, and in places had done so. Tolly had to keep his flashlight trained on the floor to see where he was treading, but across the top, cords of elm root had pushed between the stones and felt their way through space into the wall on the other side, making loops at neck height that every now and then gave him a nasty jerk. Tolly got very tired with stumbling and began to have nightmare fears. Suppose the bulging walls gave way behind him and he was trapped? Suppose there was someone or something beside himself in the tunnel? There was a most disquieting echo. Supposing the flashlight gave out? He seemed to have come a long way. The roots that crossed his path had changed. These were now yew—he knew that, because up above in the garden they showed round the trunk. They dived into the earth and surfaced and dived again and had a kind of bark that was easily recognized. So he was under or near one of the yew trees, making for the house. One yew was near St. Christopher and the old chapel and the moat. The other was nearer the part of the house that had been burned down. Was there a way out at the other end, and if so, where? Tolly was

126

eaten up with curiosity but also with panic. He desperately
wanted to be safely out again. Orlando was whining, a
nasty, upsetting little noise. The flashlight lit on still, black
water. It might be shallow, but Tolly had no stick to probe
it. Perhaps you were chased down the tunnel till you fell
into a well. Perhaps it came to river level, and when somebody opened the lock, water came in and filled up the
passage. Perhaps—Tolly's imagination became wild—octo-
pus things came out of the water. He had once seen a
film of the bed of the sea, where squids ran as swiftly
and fluently as spiders. The water and the silence pressing
on his eardrums was too much for him. He turned and
made all the speed he could, stumbling and fighting to
get back, but instead of seeming shorter, the return journey
felt endless. At one moment, resting his hand on the
cracked roof, he felt a worm wriggle and was as fright
ened as if he had touched a horridly unnatural finger. His
flashlight did give out, but while he panicked in the absolute darkness, he heard Orlando scampering upstairs ahead
of him and presently was able to distinguish a glimmering
on the desolate walls like gray dawn down the old chimney.
He lifted Orlando out and then heaved himself up with
difficulty on his arms, for the opening was too narrow to
swing up a leg. It was night in the Bower, but after the
tunnel it was easy to his eyes. He crept out thankfully into
the air. The first thing he saw was the evening star. He
had quite lost his sense of time. Down there, where there
was neither sunrise nor sunset, he might have lost days,
or, like Rip van Winkle, a hundred years. He was glad to

127

see the candlelight shining from the house. His great-grandmother must be back, and she would be wondering where he had been. He thought with pride how little she knew. Orlando streaked off toward the house and Tolly followed slowly, looking at the shapes of the trees whose boughs he knew so well and at the shape of the spaces between the trees, usually alive with birds but now they were all asleep. Everything seemed fixed in a trance of eternal sameness.

The door of the living room was open, and before he reached it, he could hear voices, very low and urgent.

Susan was sitting on the rug by the fire plucking at it with her fingers. Jacob—Tolly thought him a companion in a million—was standing beside her looking out of the window.

He had a basket in his hand. "No, Missy. If I go now, him get caught. Caxton watch all the time. He look out of every window. He go into garden, pretend to get wood, pretend to look at church clock. He know we know."

"Isn't it dark yet, Jacob?"

"Not dark enough, Missy, and moon rise early. Fred wait till Captain comes home, then he all right."

"But, Jacob, he's hungry."

"He not starve in one night. But he very frightened."

"Why are people frightened in the dark? It's silly. I ought to be frightened all the time, but I am not."

"He frightened no one come to let him out. He frightened dead man's spirit come up out of water. He frightened of snakes."

"Jacob, we can't leave him alone there without any food, not knowing what anyone is doing." Susan stopped as Tolly came in. "Who's there?"

"Nobody there, Missy."

"It's me," said Tolly.

"Ai, ai!" said Jacob, and if his hair could have stood on end, it would have. Then, suddenly, he saw Tolly.

"Who's that, Missy?"

"It's all right. He's a friend of mine. He's my cousin Toseland."

"I suppose," said Tolly, "Fred, whoever he is, is hidden in the tunnel."

"Sh! Fred is Boggis's youngest son," Susan explained. "He's in the tunnel because he was poaching and the gamekeeper caught him, but he got away. He could be hanged if he is caught now. It's Caxton's doing. Caxton gets boys to go poaching for him. He makes money out of it. He doesn't want Fred caught because he may get into trouble himself. He wants to sell him to the press gang, but if he found him in the tunnel, he might kill him and no one would ever know who did it. Jacob says Caxton knows we've hidden him."

"Mr. Jonathan bring Fred to me early this morning when I out fishing. Mr. Jonathan say, 'Jacob, you know all good hiding places. Hide Fred for me.' And Fred look frightened like him going to die. So I hide him in tunnel. He have no food all day, because Caxton always watching everywhere. He not even know we had letter that Captain comes tonight."

129

"Is that basket for him? I'll take it," said Tolly. "If Caxton comes after me, I'll—disappear." He laughed, but he hoped with all his heart it wasn't a vain boast. He picked up the basket and said, "Good-by. You'll see." And then he saw from Jacob's face that at the very word he had—disappeared. He laughed again, hoping Jacob would hear it, and went out. He turned a resolute back to the house, though well aware that there was something behind him that he didn't like to think of. The house itself felt wrong, it felt too big, smothering the darkness. He knew that Caxton's snaky eyes were watching, that if he turned he would see, perhaps downstairs, perhaps upstairs, a shape behind the glass. Or perhaps Caxton was standing in wait under the shadow of the yew tree where he must pass. Tolly's instinct told him that frightened things had a peculiar attraction for Caxton that brought them instantly to his notice, but if he could manage not to be frightened, he wouldn't be seen. So he defiantly sang at the top of his voice:

> *"O wha dare meddle wi' me*
> *O wha dare meddle wi' me?*
> *My name is little Jack Elliot*
> *And wha dare meddle wi' me?"*

The moon was rising, and but for the very peculiar circumstances that he was in, his crossing of the lawn with his own knifelike shadow underlining him must have been clearly visible.

The ruined hiding place in the shrubbery was silhouetted

130

against the sky by the moon just behind it. Its outline looked higher than he had remembered. It looked like a real tower, but perhaps part of the black mass was just ivy on the trees. And though, as anybody knows who has thought about it, feet and bodies are much cleverer and quicker in getting over rough ground in the dark than in the light, he was surprised to find his way through the bushes so easily. The moonlight shone through the window onto the floor of the Bower, which was lucky, as the flashlight was finished. Since he had left the place such a short time ago, someone had put a small stone table in the middle of the floor, and it was all roomier than he had remembered. Perhaps it was just the effect of moonlight, but it did not surprise or bother him because he was too excited to think of anything but poor Fred Boggis alone down there with the door shut on him, alone and "frightened like him going to die." Tolly could not find the trap door. He pushed the stone table aside to look under it and felt with his hands too, because moonlight is so deceptive. Where the table had stood there was an iron ring riveted to the floor. He would never have seen it, but his fingers found it. With this he easily raised the thin flagstone, but as he did so and took hold of the wooden door underneath, there was a wild scurry of boots down the stairs below. Looking down into the shadows, Tolly heard echoing footsteps as whoever it was tried to escape. He leaned over and whistled Jacob's African birdcall. The footsteps stopped and the echoes died away. There was a long silence. Tolly whistled again, and very slowly the steps

131

began to return. The moonlight fell on a boy's face, white, thin, and terrified. Tolly found it impossibly difficult to speak. He handed down the basket, on top of which he was glad to see candles and a tinder box. He watched, fascinated, while Fred, with hands shaking like an old man's, lit the candle.

"Is the Captain really coming back—*soon*?" he asked in a sobbing whisper.

Tolly nodded.

"You'd better shut that trap door again. Somebody might see the light. I don't want Caxton here. I thought you was him just now. It's better shut. But I'm glad of a candle. It's the truth the Captain's coming?"

Tolly nodded again. He lowered the wood and the stone quietly into position and pushed the table back. He felt indescribably tired, as if he were a hundred years old. It seemed too coldhearted just to go away and leave Fred. He sat down, leaning his back against the wall, and blinked at the bright moon through the window. Something was queer. The ivy stem like a monstrous caterpillar crawled through the slit window into the shrubs, but it was a window above that through which the moonlight streamed, and the roof was open to the sky. He blinked again and could not keep his eyes open; and, ceasing to care if it was dream or waking, past or present, at once he was fast asleep.

He was wakened by Orlando's whiskery face poking him in the ear and a paddy foot on his eyelid. His great-grandmother was calling him and sounded as if she had been calling a long time. He crawled out of the bushes and slipped away down the path that led to the green animals, answering her from there, because he felt like keeping his big secret a little longer.

She stood in the moonlight, a little figure leaning forward to listen, like a bird.

"Hello, Granny Partridge," he said, putting his arm through hers.

"Oh, there you are at last, Tolly. I was quite worried when I couldn't find you. Bless us, how cold your hands are! And you smell of the moat. Have you been in it?"

"Not quite," he said in a waking-up voice. "I'm terribly hungry."

"So am I. What shall we have? Grilled sausage and bacon? Go and have a bath and come back in your dressing gown. You look like a dog that has been ratting. I'll have it all ready for you by then."

Tolly came down refreshed and soapy, with shining wet hair.

"You look tall in your dressing gown. It's quite like having a man in the house. I *enjoy* having a man about the place. We'll have a *tête-à-tête* supper on the little table by the fire. The weather's breaking. I feel it in my bones."

When the supper was set before them, Orlando's nose wiggled like a tongue, but the grilled sausage and bacon couldn't have tasted better to him than it did to Tolly. Afterwards there was apple pie and some chocolates that Mrs. Oldknow had brought, and then Tolly stretched himself out in the armchair with his bedroom slippers on the fender and his hands behind his head. All through supper he was bursting to tell her that he had *been back to them*, but either he couldn't or he wouldn't. It never got said. Mrs. Oldknow kept looking at him with her laughing black eyes that had wrinkles like a series of croquet hoops above them, dividing her forehead into patterns. There was a long silence, broken only by Orlando barking in his dreams. His mouth was shut and the barks puffed up his cheeks and came out in little melancholy explosions. Tolly laughed, put a fourth chocolate in his mouth, and said, "Did Captain Oldknow come home when he was expected?"

"Not often. There were so many comings and goings. But there was one time—it was in 1798. I remember it because of the things that happened afterwards.

⋖§ THE CAPTAIN'S RETURN §⋗

He had been away for months in London with Maria instead of a fortnight, but he came back the same day that the letter announcing his coming arrived. Susan was waiting up for him, dressed by Betsy in frills and fal-lals such as she had not worn since Nanny Softly fell ill. Jacob also was in his best suit, very solemn, but they were both equally joyful. In those days an arrival was a real and prolonged excitement. Instead of a mere sweep of headlights, so dazzling in their approach as to make everything else invisible, and the brisk slam of a car door, there was first the clatter of the postilion's hooves on the gravel to announce that the chaise was following. Then the wonderful moment of certain expectation when everyone ran out with lanterns. The chaise was heard bowling up the drive and the leading horses came into the swinging lantern light, and it shone fierily on wheels and windows, on horses and grooms and footmen, and on the ladies being handed out by gentlemen. But to Susan all this commotion was in sound. She heard the hubbub of well-known voices and the patter of recognizable steps going this way and that, her grandmother's stick and little cough, the clamor in the kitchen before the green baize door swung to and cut it off. She heard the thrilling change from trot to walk of the four horses and the gravel falling off the wheels like water off a water wheel, dying away as they slowed down. She heard the coachman put up his whip in its socket, the reins flap on the horses backs, the grooms run forward to the horses, who were stretching their necks and shaking their heads in a jingle of harness as they relaxed after the long pull, the creak of springs and the opening door. She smelled the hot metal of the lanterns, the sweat of the horses, the leather polish on the harness, and when the chaise door was opened, the always unlikable smell of the inside of any kind of carriage.

Sefton was there and Jonathan and his father, Mr. Morley, and indoors the maids were lined up to curtsy. Susan had gone out with Jonathan, and she curtsied to her mother, as little girls should, and said, "Welcome, Mama,"

and was offered a cheek to kiss in an aura of perfume and a rustle of silk. And then her father was there.

They all went in, for the parson and Jonathan were to stay for dinner, late though it was. Everyone was greeted, including all the servants. Maria was laughingly gracious over that part of the occasion. She was convinced they adored her—in fact Caxton had frequently made so bold as to tell her so. News was exchanged, but though the Captain was apparently giving his attention to his old friend Morley, he was really watching Susan and hardly able to take in what he saw. She was a different child. Her face was round and happy, and though she was holding his hand, it was not the clutch of dependence. He even had the impression that as she leaned against him she was searching for someone else.

"What are you unquiet about, my love?"

"You haven't spoken to Jacob, Papa."

"Bless me! Where is that little scamp? Jacob!!"

"I am willing to bet that he is no farther away than outside the door," said Jonathan. "May I fetch him?"

Jacob was very conscious of the occasion, and his cheeks were high and round with delight.

"Good evening, Jacob."

Jacob bowed low, lower even than Caxton. "Good evening, sir."

"I am sorry I missed seeing you, Jacob, when I arrived."

"His face didn't show in the dark," Sefton cut in. "He was there, hopping about like a cat on hot bricks."

"I have not had an account of you yet from Mr. Jonathan, but as far as I can judge from Miss Susan, you have looked after her extremely well."

"Papa," said Susan, tugging at him with impatience, "may I have dinner with you tonight? I can feed myself quite well now. Jacob taught me. We have our meals together since Nanny Softly has been ill."

"Yes, Captain," Jacob nodded. "Miss Susan eat very well. I teach her all manners what Cook teach me. Not drink soup from bowl, not eat peas with knife. Miss Susan eat so refined like Cook."

Everybody laughed and Susan wriggled, but at least the Captain and Jonathan and his father laughed kindly.

"Those *will* be lovely table manners," said Maria. "The best in the county."

"Well done, Jacob. That is good to hear. Maria, my love, if you agree, Susan shall join us tonight. She can sit

137

at the end of the table beside Jonathan, and Jacob shall be her personal butler."

Maria and Sefton checked their high spirits long enough for her to say, "As you wish, my love. By all means let us have a family party."

"This is all Betsy's doing," croaked the grandmother. "I had no idea of it, or you may be sure I should not have allowed it. I have *very serious* things to tell you about Jacob."

"Let us leave that until after dinner, Ma'am. Susan will like to hear about our stay in London, and news is never so interesting at the second telling. Caxton, will you set a place for Miss Susan next to Mr. Jonathan, and Jacob will wait on her."

(Tolly was listening to all this with some impatience, hugging his knees and grinning secretly. He wanted to get on to the next part of the story.)

After supper, while Maria was telling her London gossip to Sefton (the only person really interested in fashion, snobbery, and scandal) and the parson was listening politely to something that had shocked the grandmother in somebody else's behavior, Captain Oldknow gave Susan the present he had bought for her. This time it was the coral necklace and bracelet that you found upstairs. Susan was enchanted. She put on the bracelet and shook her wrist to feel it slide cool and loose there. She felt now as special and feminine as her mother.

"Let me look at your hand, Sue. You have a ring on your finger. Who gave you that?"

"I found it, Papa. It was in the dough. We asked the miller if anyone had lost it, but he said no." Whatever Susan guessed about the ring, she only said the truth. "May I keep it, Papa?"

"Why, yes. It is very pretty. But if you ever hear who it belongs to, you must give it back."

"I wonder," the grandmother said, "that you are at such pains to teach Susan vanity—the one sin that her blindness mercifully makes almost impossible for her."

"Forgive me, Ma'am. I should be disappointed in my daughter if she were not a little vain. She knows I see her with pleasure. Let me put the necklace on you myself, Sue."

Susan bent her neck to keep her curls away from the clasp while he fumbled with it. She heard the door close as Caxton went out with the tray. Then she whipped round and clasped her father round the neck to kiss him ardently in thanks, and under cover of this prolonged embrace she whispered urgently in his ear.

"*What?* Say that again."

(Tolly's feet came down to the floor with a thump. "I wondered however much longer they were going to leave poor Fred Boggis alone in the tunnel. I know he had candles, but, Granny, he was *scared*."

Mrs. Oldknow stopped abruptly in her sewing, her needle held motionless in mid-air, and looked fixedly at

Tolly. He couldn't have wished her to be more surprised. Then she relaxed, laughing.

"I might have known it was you! I was going to tell you about the strange boy who came in the nick of time and was never seen again. I always thought it was Alexander."

"I was ME," said Tolly triumphantly. "I found the tunnel this morning, and the rest happened—I was going to say this evening, but it doesn't seem to make sense, does it? I was on guard at the top and Fred was underneath, and I fell asleep. And then you called me. But go on. Susan whispered in his ear—")

The Captain seemed to consider a moment; his eyes wandered over the people in the room as if wondering whether to trust them. Sefton? His charming, careless, frivolous wife? His fierce old mother? The parson and Jonathan—yes, these two certainly. But here was Caxton again with logs for the fire, so all he said was, "Very well, Sue, my love. Leave it to me," and to Caxton, "Send in Jacob for a moment."

Jacob was hanging about for possible glimpses of his idol, the Captain, when the door opened, and he dived under Caxton's elbow and presented himself.

"Come here, Jacob. I didn't forget you when I was in London. I brought you a present too." He fished in his pocket for a parcel while Susan bounced and clicked her heels together with pleasure. Jacob received a new razor-sharp jackknife with two blades, a scoop and a point. His smile nearly reached his ears.

"Now I carve Miss Susan a beautiful box for her and make many things."

"He made me a drum with rabbit skin; it made a humming drumming noise and I liked it, but Grandmama said it was wicked and she put her heel through it."

"You must know," said the grandmother with her bitter croaking voice, "that Jacob was practicing heathen idolatries in front of St. Christopher, and your daughter was actually beating out the devilish rhythms for his dancing. After all the pains I have taken to teach her religion, you, my son, introduce a black savage to lead her straight to damnation."

"Jonathan gave him a good thrashing for it anyway," said Sefton. "I was surprised. I always thought Jonathan was soft. The noise! He must have lammed him properly. Certainly I never heard a noise like that when I was at school."

Jacob's eyes rolled toward Jonathan, but their faces never twitched.

"Susan had her hands caned too," said the grandmother. "She showed no repentance."

Captain Oldknow opened Susan's pink hands and saw the marks across them. He hid them between his own and his face was sad.

"It was only a childish game," he said.

"No, sir, not game." Jacob was very honest.

"Of course it was in play. There was no sense in it. But this is a Christian country and such games give offence. I blame myself for his ignorance, Morley. He should

141

have proper instruction. Will you spare some time in the evenings for him? He can come round to the parsonage."

Mr. Morley readily agreed.

"Jacob, you can go into my study now. Wait there for me. I will come and talk to you when the ladies have gone upstairs."

Jacob looked anxiously at Susan, but of course she couldn't see that. Some thought, however, passed from one to the other. She clasped her hands and twiddled her thumbs, the signal they had arranged for "All's Well."

"Good night, Jacob."

Jacob went out with a certain jauntiness.

It was not long before the grandmother and Susan went upstairs, and Sefton joined his mother in her boudoir where they laughed together, making fun of everyone and everything, from which not even the Captain was excepted. But there were a great many things that Sefton kept even from his mother, particularly the shady and disgraceful dealings in which Caxton took part.

Meanwhile, in the study, Jacob, confirmed by Jonathan, was telling all that he knew about the gang of boys that Caxton employed as poachers for his own profit. Fred Boggis was thirteen and strong for his age. When the keeper caught him, he struggled and got away, owing to the keeper's catching his foot in a bramble and stumbling. The laws against poaching were very severe, and for fighting with a keeper a boy could be hanged. Jacob knew Caxton's activities in selling victims to the press gang,

142

but he did not mention this in case the Captain, as a naval officer, approved of it.

("I wanted to ask you what the press gang was," Tolly interrupted.

"It was a roving gang that kidnaped men for the Navy. There were not enough sailors for the fleet, and without the fleet the French could not be defeated. So this dreadful way of getting them was allowed. Captain Oldknow detested it and would never himself have been satisfied with unwilling sailors. But it was not to ships like his that they were sent, but those that had a bad name and so could not get men.")

What Jacob did not know was that Sefton was concerned in this nasty trade as well as Caxton, and this very night they had arranged the capture of a band of local youths who were going to the fair at Downham Market. Sefton had been out all day on his horse and only Caxton knew where. And here I may as well tell you that unknown to Sefton, Caxton had long plans. It suited him that Sefton was getting daily further into debt, gambling in the hope of putting it right before his father found out. He went horse racing, using money lent him by Caxton to put on horses that Caxton knew were certain winners. But somehow they never won. Caxton hoped that the war would not end before the Captain was killed. He imagined himself with such a hold over Sefton that in the end all the money would be in his own pocket. Then he could marry the

143

wretched Susan and take over the family house. If necessary, he might even marry Maria, but that would be tiresome. He need never take any notice of Susan. He could get rid of her.

The Captain, however, could not guess at so much hidden villainy. The ruin of Fred Boggis was enough to decide him that Caxton must be dismissed. The Captain and Jacob went to bring out poor Fred, the parson was sent to tell Boggis and his wife and bring them to say good-by to their son, and Jonathan went to hire a post chaise to wait for them outside the village. Then Fred was bundled in with the parson and driven off to Portsmouth, to the *Woodpecker*, and enrolled as part of the crew, where he would be under the Captain's protection. This done, the Captain joined Maria and Sefton, still gossiping upstairs, without their knowing that anything had been going on.

❦

"Do you think you could find the tunnel again?" Mrs. Oldknow asked Tolly at breakfst next day.

"Of course I can. At least, I hope so. It's under the floor of that old ruin. It's all very puzzling. You see, when I went back to Fred, it was different. Only somehow I didn't really notice."

"Different—Tolly, I'm thrilled. Hand me that album, please. That one, on the window seat. I keep cuttings and pictures about the house in it. Look—"

144

She pointed out a photograph of a painting. It was a night scene showing the end of the garden, not very much altered, except that on the skyline among bushes there was a ruined, roofless tower hung with ivy and traveler's-joy. A low moon was shining through the upper window.

"This was painted in 1806. In those days ruins were the thing. Every large garden had to have one to make a romantic prospect. If there wasn't one, it had to be made. We were lucky in having a real one, though nobody knows what it was originally built for, and it gradually crumbled away."

Tolly hung over this picture without saying anything. It was queer to see a photograph of his dreams.

"I should like to see it, Tolly. You must take me there."

"You would have to crawl quite a long way. Do you mind?"

Tolly led her to the jungle of bushes through which he had made a hole such as a tiger might make pushing through to its lair.

"I could cut it bigger," he offered reluctantly.

"I think that would spoil it. Bring me a mackintosh to put over my head. I hate having my scalp caught in brambles."

Tolly brought her mackintosh, which was a brown and black check, and bent double with this over her head and her sharp eyes peeping out, Granny Partridge went gamely in, any difficulty she had being expressed in clucks and tchks that are common to old ladies and birds.

145

"Do you know, Tolly," she said when they had arrived in the Bower and she was sitting on a stone, "I have never been here in my life before, only heard of it, and never believed it. I expect the tunnel ends under the old chapel. The Bower would make a good hiding place for a priest. He could come up out of the tunnel to take the air. Next holidays I will invite some friends who are archaeologists to stay, and we will try to find the other end. You shall be the first one down any hole they find, I promise you. I don't suppose you will mind a little water."

"I mind octopuses."

"My dear child! You have been reading about the Abominable Snowman and the Cealocanth and the Giant Red-Haired Lion! This tunnel isn't prehistoric, connecting with a hidden sea. It can't be older than Elizabeth or James I. The best you can hope for is a skeleton or two."

This was certainly something to look forward to.

"Aren't you coming down the tunnel?"

"I think not. I should hate to smell as musty as you did last night. I should feel like a mummy. Take me up the river in a punt. Let's look for kingfishers."

The holidays were slipping past as smoothly and relentlessly as the river.

"What a quantity of new dress stuffs Maria brought back from London!" Mrs. Oldknow ruminated as she rummaged in her patchwork baskets. "And of course she was determined to show them off to the whole county. And that brings me to tonight's story, which I will call—"

❦ THE "WOODPECKER'S" RIGGING ❧

After being away from home for so long, Captain Oldknow had many things to see to on his estate, and many visits to pay to friends and relations. He had said nothing to Maria or to Caxton about dismissing the latter, because he hoped to hear among his neighbors of another more reliable man to take his place.

When they went visiting, usually he and Sefton rode and Maria and the grandmother went in the carriage. Susan of course was left behind. Her father would have taken her when they were going to houses where there were children, but Maria never would.

"All children are nuisances," she said. "And what pleasure could there be in visiting if I have to hold Susan by the hand all the time and be continually apologizing for her? There is nothing so tedious as parents talking about their children."

For Susan there were compensations. She begged Cook to make turnovers for supper, and before they were cooked, she wrote names on the pastry—Apple, Apricot, Plum—to surprise her father. This she was allowed to do in lesson time while Jacob was writing on his slate.

In the afternoons there was a new excitement. Jacob

had finished his ivy rope ladder and had fastened it to the branch of a tree, and Susan was going up the rigging of the *Woodpecker* in imagination and sitting astride the boom. Jacob had the intelligence to see that a person who could not see would not be afraid of height. He taught her to climb and watched over her with the greatest care. She was handicapped by her long clinging frocks, which were always in the way, getting under her feet or catching on the wood. Jacob fetched his old white cotton pantaloons that the Captain had bought him in Barbados, and he made Susan put them on, stuffing her dress inside and hitching them round her waist with a red handkerchief. This was an unheard-of thing for little girls in those days, but Susan didn't know what clothes looked like and Jacob didn't know what little girls could or could not do. So they were both perfectly happy. There was no one to see them. Boggis was in the kitchen garden setting potatoes. Betsy was taking the opportunity when the ladies were away to read Maria's novels. Old Mrs. Softly had gone home to her sister's for a change.

Each time Susan ventured one hold higher up a tree, Jacob carved her initial on the bark, which she of course could recognize when she climbed there again. She did the yew trees first, because they were easier, almost like spiral staircases. She loved the feel of their drooping leaves, something like a horse's mane, the scaly bark that rattled under her hand, and the pungent scent that grew stronger as she went up. And a feeling of being above and away from the earth she certainly had, rocking in freedom

148

on a high fork and hearing birds passing below her.

Generally the two of them came down to tidy themselves before the family were due back. Jacob hid the white pantaloons in the Bower and Susan shook out the crumpled feeling in her dress and picked the twigs and leaves out of her hair. Then well pleased with themselves they went in to wash.

One day it happened that the carriage returned earlier than expected, when the children were up the tree. Susan heard the familiar wheels first, and both of them came scrambling down. Susan was still in the bottom branches when her father and mother came strolling into the garden.

"What boy is that playing with Jacob? He should be looking after Susan, not climbing trees with boys picked up in the village." The Captain's frown changed to a look of unbelief as Susan, dropping from the tree, came running toward him calling, "Papa, Papa," as loud as any thrush.

"It is your ladylike little daughter and her enterprising black escort," said Maria, amused at her husband's disconcerted face. "If only Grandmother were here to see! But it is just as well she is not. I fear she would die of a stroke."

"Papa," said Susan, clasping him round the legs before he had made up his mind what to say. "Will you take me some day in the *Woodpecker*? I can climb riggings. I have been right up to the top royal gallant. Jacob says so."

"Miss Susan climb like cat. Very clever hands and feet and not afraid ever."

The Captain was silent. His heart stopped at the thought

149

of Susan falling. And yet, while he had known nothing about it, she had learned, and her face was shining with pride. He could have thrashed Jacob for letting her risk it. He could have embraced him for teaching her freedom.

"Shall I do it for you, Papa?" Susan put out her hand to catch the drooping leaves of the endmost spray of yew by which she could guide herself toward the trunk.

"Yes, my love. *Jacob*!" he said agonizingly.

"You see, Captain. Miss Susan climb well. I make her wear pantaloons to be safe."

"Just look at the back of them! What a sight. And how you, my dear husband, can bear to look on while she breaks her neck is quite beyond me. I shall never understand you. You always profess to be so devoted to her. But if you don't mind her being nearly as black as Jacob and quite immodest, perhaps I am really the one who cares most, for I should be ashamed for anyone to see her."

The Captain was watching Susan with more fear than he had ever felt in battle, but he saw after a while that she was no more likely to fall than anybody else.

"Papa!" she called from the upper branches. "There's a tit's nest here. I can feel the eggs. They are warm. But those sea gulls you can hear are not real. It's only Jacob. He always does sea gulls for me when I am playing ship."

"Well done, Midshipman Susan," her father said when she was safely down. "You have certainly earned a trip on the *Woodpecker*. But your pantaloons are badly torn." He laid a grateful hand on Jacob's shoulder and shook it gently, unable to say anything to him.

"Go in now and make yourself as nice as your mother likes to see you, and join us in the parlor. 'For desperate ills, desperate remedies,' " he said to Maria. "Since she is blind, she must be allowed some things that would not be usual for a young lady. The pantaloons were a wise precaution and do not offend me at her age. There will be time enough for her to be elegant and sedate."

"You are out of date, my dear husband, as well as out of touch from seeing nothing but oceans. Since the French Revolution, nobody believes in the Age of Innocence. It is quite out of fashion."

⋞§⋟

Tolly had spent an afternoon helping Boggis with a bonfire of spring prunings and rubbish. There was a lively wind, so that when, after long coaxing with newspaper and paraffin, the fire took hold and rose in a crackling pillar, not only the smoke would suddenly veer and cut his sight and breath, but sheets of flame coiled sideways and took off, landing on nearby bushes that sparkled and frizzled like singed hair, or even caught fire and held a candle flame on each twig's end until it died out on the more sappy wood. Or the fire snaked away among grass and dead leaves and had to be trampled out. The cherry trees were in full blossom, but the sky behind them was heavy with slate and indigo clouds, and the smoke hung low and wound itself round everything in the garden.

151

Tolly almost expected the Green Deer to sneeze and the Green Hare to lollop off.

He came in with his imagination full of fire.

"Tell me about the house being burned down, please, Granny. It is so very difficult to get a bonfire started, I can't think how houses start."

"Very often they have to be helped."

"Who would want to set fire to a house? Except enemies."

"Well, enemies, to start with. Anyway, it happens often enough for there to be a special word for it—arson. But I'll tell you."

⋙ THE FIRE ⋘

The Captain had to go back to Portsmouth to see how the repairs to the *Woodpecker* were going on and the preparations for putting to sea, and at the same time to bring news of Fred to his parents. He had dismissed Caxton, who was to be replaced by someone he could trust. Had he known how bad Caxton really was, he might not have dismissed him when he was going to be absent himself. Poaching was not in his eyes a deadly sin, but it was a thing a gentleman could not condone because it spoiled his neighbors' sport. As for Fred, boys will always poach whether they are urged to or not. But seeing that he was away himself for such long periods, it was essential that

152

the manservant should be irreproachable. Maria made a great fuss about losing Caxton, who had been there a long time and satisfied her ideas of style. Also she was threatened with losing her cook too, whom Caxton had long flattered with hints of marriage, though as you know he had other grander ideas. Sefton was really frightened because of the money he owed him. He thought it best to get out of the way as quickly as possible, and surprised and pleased his father by asking to be allowed to go with him to see the *Woodpecker*, and to go straight on from Portsmouth to Oxford where he was to begin his studies. They went off together early in the morning. Caxton was to leave the next day. Jonathan gave Susan and Jacob a holiday to cheer her up after her father had gone, and he took them both for a long day on the river. This was the first time Susan had been in a sailing boat. Meanwhile, Maria, who did not believe in moping, was going off for the day to a neighbor's housewarming, driven by one of the elegant young men who were always at her command. She had the pleasure of the very stylish carriage and four horses that you see in the picture, and a dashing driver. She was to bring a party back with her to finish up the day's pleasure at Green Knowe. This was why she had insisted on Caxton's staying an extra day after her husband had gone.

It was on her return, when the house was full of her guests, that she discovered the loss of her jewels. The cases were all there, but empty. You can imagine the uproar. There was no police force in those days—only a village constable who could make an arrest if somebody else caught the thief for him. The doors were locked while the house was searched and the servants questioned, the guests all helping and finding it better entertainment than they could have hoped for. Only Maria was distracted, beyond even enjoying having her young gentleman's supporting arm round her. Susan was in bed, wondering what the excitement could be. She was now, at her father's suggestion, to have a room of her own, and while the night nursery was being done up for her, she slept in a little room at the top of the old house that was then reached by the main staircase in the new part. Both the staircases were in fact outside the old walls, one on each side. Maria's parties were often noisy with laughter and flirtatious scutters, but not with so much coming and going up and down from top to bottom.

The rooms and the servants were searched in vain. Caxton was foremost in helping and most willingly allowed a search of his room and his newly packed baggage and his pockets. He suggested that Jacob was a likely thief, but Jacob had been with Jonathan all day and was still at the parsonage having his religious instruction with Mr. Morley. No trace of anything was found, and at last with Maria, Cook, and Betsy in tears, the grandmother sermonizing in her most irritating style, and Caxton sublimely efficient, supper was served. Maria, holding her smelling salts in one hand, was able to take a little soup. But the guests, full of talk, excitement, and even laughter, fell to with good appetites and more than usual thirst. The theft might have been laid on specially for their pleasure. Everyone had a theory and was prepared to argue loudly about it.

In the middle of the poultry course, a loud shriek from Betsy was almost unheard except by Caxton, who went out to see what was the matter, leaving the door ajar. He did not at once return, but an oily, choking smell filtered into the dining room that was not, could not be, burned food. Then Caxton came in very white and regretted to say that the drawing room was on fire. From the kitchen came hysterical shouts of "Fire! Fire!" and somebody began pealing the coachman's bell. Everybody leaped up from the table and ran out. Maria did not choose her friends for their sense, and though the gentlemen tried to help by throwing buckets of water on the flames, there was no one to take command and only confusion resulted. If the Captain had been at home, perhaps the fire could have been checked, but very soon it had taken hold and nothing could be done. You must remember they had neither telephones nor fire engines, as we know them, and no water upstairs.

Jacob had finished his lesson with Mr. Morley and said good night. He opened the parsonage door and saw the sky black-red like a dark rose, and a bitter smell cut his breath. Flakes of white ash floated on the wind, and the night was full of sounds like a battle, a land battle with screaming horses. As he stood sniffing and frightened, beyond the trees a column of dense crimson smoke went up in a spiral and spread in rolling coils above a frenzy of flame and shooting sparks. He turned and hammered on the door.

"Mr. Morley, Mr. Jonathan, Green Knowe is burning!"

155

They all came running, and on the way met a man come to
fetch them. Everybody from the village was there, men,
women, and children. It was difficult to break the ring of
watchers to get in where round the house figures black
like dancing devils against the glare worked to save what
they could. From the house furniture and pictures were
being carried out, bedding thrown from the windows.
Everybody was shouting—they had to, to be heard above
the roar and pistol shots of the fire.

"It's on both sides of the house," yelled Jonathan. "Both
staircases."

"Where's Missy? Where's Miss Susan?" Jacob shot off

like a dog, searching the different groups of people for her.
"Where's Missy? Where's Miss Susan?"

Maria was fainting on a sofa in the garden surrounded
by friends. He could get no answer.

Betsy and the kitchenmaid were carrying away pillows,
blankets, and clothes tossed out of the first floor windows
by Boggis.

"Where's Missy, Betsy? Where's Miss Susan?"

But Betsy was trying to hear what Boggis was shouting
about the stairs burning.

"Can't stay no longer—get out while I can."

"Betsy, where's Missy?"

"Miss Susan? With her grandmother I don't doubt."

The old lady was sitting bolt upright on a small gilt
chair under a tree among a pile of books out of the study.
Both her hands rested on the knob of her cane, and a look
of triumphant piety sharpened her witchlike face as she
watched the leaping, eating flames.

"Where's Miss Susan, Ma'am?"

"Susan? Susan will be with Betsy. He shall burn up the
chaff with unquenchable fire," she said.

Jacob ran on, his heart feeling bigger than his whole
body. As he went round the house, he saw Caxton beating
off Cook, who was trying to hold him back from the
main door. Jacob could see in, through gaps in the swirling
smoke, to the burning staircase. The banisters and handrail
were crackling and curling. Flames perched and flew
away and perched again, until fed by bubbles of boiling
paint they settled into a hedge of fire. Even so, edging

against the wall, it might be possible to pass, and Caxton, pulling his coat over his head, rushed in, leaving Cook wailing.

"Where's Missy?"

But Cook only cried, "He'll never get through—he'll never—"

At the front of the house a crowd of men stood under Susan's high bedroom window. Some held a blanket, and all together they shouted at regular intervals, "Jump! Jump! Jump!"

Jacob found Mr. Morley and Jonathan holding the blanket, as distressed as he was himself. Up on the top floor Susan stood by the window. Her room was inside the old house, and the fire had not passed the three-foot stone walls, but it was traveling along the roof. From outside one could see flames like antlers thrusting through the slates. Smoke was billowing out of her window that she had opened for air. She had been to the top of the staircase and called, but no one had heard. The blast of heat was so dreadful and the whole position so unknown that she could do nothing but go back into her room and shut the door to keep some of the heat and smoke out.

"Oh, Susan, jump!"

But Susan could not, nor is that surprising. She could hear the shouts, but the fire was as loud as an express train. She could neither recognize the hoarse voices nor tell for certain where they were. Her room was suffocating and the whole house felt madly alive, groaning and trembling and rocked with explosions; but there was no flame yet in her room to drive her out and she could not see the danger from the roof.

"Where's the ladder?" Jacob shouted.

"It's not here. It was lent to the farmer."

Jacob took in the situation.

"I'll bring her. Down the chimney. Come, Mr. Jonathan." Jacob had crossed the Atlantic in a wooden battleship and had certainly seen fire drill. He seized towels from a heap of linen and dipped them in a bucket, one to tie round his mouth and one for Susan. He dragged Jonathan into the dining room, told him to bring a blanket there, and made for the chimney from which smoke and hot ash were pouring. Jonathan gave him a leg up and away he went. The chimney, being in the center of the old house was, compared with the bedlam all round, quieter by isolation and cooler, though still stifling. The roar from the roof came down through the distant opening at the top, and as he climbed up and the shouts of the crowd were cut off, he heard the terrifying whistling hum of sheet flame beyond the walls. It grew hotter as he went up. He reached the iron door that led to the space under the roof. The metal blistered his fingers as he pushed it open. The noise was instantly deafening and the heat stunning. He ran, pouring with sweat, to the iron door that he calculated should lead to Susan's flue and slid down. He arrived almost immediately in her fireplace. Her room was full of smoke, and tongues of fire were shooting down between the slats of the ceiling. Her window curtains were blazing. He could not tell at first if she was still

159

there or still conscious. He found her crouching on the floor like a rabbit trapped in a field fire.

"Oh, Jacob! I knew you'd come."

Jacob tied the wet towel round Susan's face.

"Come, Missy, quickly. Top deck on fire, like battle. We go below. We make companion ladder of chimney. Crawl, Missy."

It was easy squirming up her little flue, harder to guide her along the joists in the scorching fog of smoke and the clatter of falling tiles, but she followed him with confidence. He lowered himself into the main chimney, straddling and bracing his back against the wall to support her as she climbed in feet first and began the descent. If it seems impossible for her to have done it, you must remember that this black chimney was no blacker, no more frightening—except for the noise and heat—than her ordinary world. She did not see the drop nor the difficulties to come. Here, just as in a tree, she must feel for finger and foothold and balance, and unlike Jacob, she could shut her eyes against the smarting smoke and hot sparks without any disadvantage. It was Jacob, always braced to take the weight if she should slip, imagining the result to them both if either should be helpless with coughing, guiding her feet and telling her what to do (for which he had to abandon his wet towel)—Jacob with a red-hot fragment in his hair that he had no free hand to brush away—who had the anguish and the anxiety. But when at last they reached the wide and really difficult part of the chimney, Jonathan was there with three men and a blanket to catch them, and they had but to drop one after the other and be carried into the open air. Both were peppered with little burns. Jacob had no hair and a nasty burn on his scalp. Mr. Morley and Jonathan took them home, where Mrs. Morley washed and bandaged and mothered them and put them both to bed in her children's room. Mr. Morley wrote a letter to the Captain and sent it off by special messenger on horseback.

Very soon after, the roof of the big new wing collapsed, falling in with a volcano of flame, and that was the climax of the fire. After that it flickered and revived and glowed and died down again for hours and hours. Yet it did not pass the thick inner walls. In the old house only Susan's bedroom ceiling fell in, but the new wings on either side were gone.

When the excitement was over, Maria's guests, having enjoyed it immensely, offered their condolences and collected their carriages, which, together with the horses belonging to the house, had been driven to a safe distance. Maria and the grandmother accepted the invitation to go home in one of the carriages and stay there till the Captain came back to make arrangements for them. Susan and Jacob were to stay with the Morleys. And very happy they were there, treated as special guests.

In the morning they went back together to the scene of the fire, hand in hand because Susan could no longer be sure of her way where underfoot it was so trampled and scarred. Jacob's head was in a regal turban of white bandage.

The servants had been busy since dawn moving the

161

salvaged furniture from the garden into sheds, barns, and coach houses. There was a dreadful mess everywhere, and fallen timber was still smouldering on the ground. The two new wings were blackened skeleton walls with holes for windows, behind which was nothing but wood charred into mosaics, piles of dirty rubbish, which but yesterday had been household treasures, and bitter smelling ash.

"Ai, Missy! Only very narrow stone house left. Big Juju man stand on guard there by wall, ivy all burned off, all black now like me."

"It's *St. Christopher*, Jacob."

"That name too hard, Missy. But he stand on guard."

They went in at the living-room door that was swinging on one hinge. Susan put her hand on the window ledge.

"Ugh! It's dirty. It feels like the chimney."

"Room all over soot, just like chimney."

"Ugh!!"

"You not mind soot last night."

"I hate it now, though. My mouth was full of it."

⋙⋘

Tolly wanted to know what happened to Caxton.

"He was never seen again. People said he must have gone back to fetch the jewels from where he had hidden them. If so, he either got away with them or he was suffocated in the fire. It seems likely that if all his wicked schemes had fallen through, he would have taken the jewels instead. Certainly he didn't set the house on fire if he had hidden the jewels in it. But it must have been set on fire by some-one because it started in two places at once, on different sides, and it smelled of oil. After a while, when rumors of Caxton's many misdeeds began to be told in the village, most people thought that the fire was started in revenge for the young men whom Sefton and Caxton had sold to the press gang. But of course nobody gave away the name of the family who did it. The only person who was pleased about the fire was Sefton, because with Caxton gone his father need never know about the money he had borrowed from him, nor about the press gang. There was enough to confess without that."

"I do hope Caxton's ghost isn't here," said Tolly.

"Nobody's bothering to keep his memory alive. Certainly not I."

The holidays were rushing to a close. They seemed to Tolly to have been full of pleasure and excitement. He could not bear the idea of going away again. But it was already the last day but one, the last day on which he would not have to say, "Tomorrow—"

He spent the day reclimbing the trees in a kind of good-by. He lolled in the top branches and studied the house from above and from the side, trying to imagine what it had been before the fire and how people could have passed from the old part to the new. There were patches of plaster, where once doors might have been, now bricked up. There were stone window sills jutting out close under the gable that showed how it must once have been higher. Was it from up there that Susan couldn't jump?

But though it was fascinating to wonder how the house had been, he did not want it different, ever, from what it was now. Its narrow ark shape was just right. His great-grandmother had said the old part was kept for children and servants and all the grand rooms were in the new wings. Where then could Caxton's bedroom have been?

When he had looked at the house long enough to remember it forever, he began to climb slowly down. The day after tomorrow was the end. He wished he could meet Susan and Jacob once more before he left. Where would they be likely to be? There was never any way of telling.

He remembered that Boggis had not yet been told about the tunnel, so he called Orlando and set off to find Boggis. Boggis straightened up, with his hand on the small of his back, and came willingly.

"When I was a boy, they always said there was a tunnel somewhere. And why should they say so if there hadn't never been one? Somebody must have knowed once. Whatever made you think of looking there?"

"Orlando dug a hole and fell through." Tolly went down as if the tunnel was now quite an ordinary thing that belonged to him, but Boggis went slowly and gingerly, feeling at every step. He seemed to be thinking less that the roof might fall in than that he might fall through the floor.

"You don't know what's underneath you. It would be a nasty thing to be shut up in here. Whatever can they have wanted a place like this for? Nothing decent and above-board, I'll be bound. Nobody wouldn't hear if you hol-

165

lered. Not down here they wouldn't." A little farther on he began again. "How would you feel if you met a swarm of rats down here? There's a chicken bone, see. Must have been rats."

Tolly was so cock-a-hoop he was beyond being frightened. If there was to be any frightening, he was going to do it.

"That's not chicken bones, Boggis. It's *human fingers*." Wouldn't that startle the boys whom he was going to invite here at half-term! He would get them scared with made-up stuff, but it would be no good telling them about Fred. They would believe any blood-curdling stories, but not the simple truth. Anyway it was his tunnel, "And wha' dare meddle wi' me."

"I wonder you're not frightened down here," Boggis went on. "It's like a grave. Smells like it too. I wouldn't come down here alone at night, not if you gave me five bob I wouldn't."

"You wouldn't know if it was night or not—it couldn't be any darker."

"Maybe. But I'm going back to my 'taties."

"What did the Captain do when he came back?" This question of Tolly's was answered with:

⋖§ THE STORY OF THE GYPSIES §⋗

Captain Oldknow was so happy to see Susan playing in the

garden with Jacob that nothing mattered in comparison. He was so pleased with Jacob and so afraid Susan might be nervous and have fire nightmares that he made them a promise. Just as soon as he had made plans with the builders, he would take them both with him in the *Woodpecker*, which was to make a peaceful cruise from Portsmouth to Bristol along the coast. You can imagine their excitement.

He had of course lost a great deal of money, because houses were not insured in those days. He could not afford to build Maria another large house. He made arrangements for a new roof to be put on the old house and new kitchens built, and saw no reason why they could not be comfortable and happy in the house as we know it now, if only Maria could be content to live quietly with fewer servants. He liked its age and its atmosphere.

"You have such a love of Gothic ruins," he said to Maria, "but which of your friends lives in anything as romantic as this? It would be perfect for Cymbeline or Tristram and Iseult."

But Maria only sulked and sulked, and instead of laughing all the time, she now only laughed at her husband with the friends with whom she was staying.

One of these was a woman as silly as herself.

"Maria," she said, "away with melancholy! There is a gypsy woman in the caravans on the common who is fabulously clever at telling fortunes. My neighbor lost her little pug dog, and for only two gold sovereigns the gypsy told her where to find it. Let us two go off by ourselves and

167

ask the gypsy about your jewels. It will be quite an adventure. We need not tell anybody."

Off they went, heavily veiled so that they should not be recognized and taking two menservants in case the gypsies should be violent. They drove in a smart carriage with four horses, a coachman and a groom—four men in all. The gypsies could hardly fail to know that they were rich and silly and that their veils were only play-acting, as the servants' livery could be seen by all.

The caravans—like little wooden chalets on high cart wheels, gaily carved and painted and ready to move off at a moment's notice—were drawn up on the edge of a wood, the horses tethered near. A dozen fierce-looking dogs rushed out, and a crowd of scowling men and thieving quicksilver children gathered in a circle round the ladies, who hesitated to advance even with their two footmen. The gypsies said nothing, except to the dogs, but every now and then a child smiled, showing all its teeth, and it did not make them any more at ease. The ladies asked for Mrs. Magda, and immediately there was a hubbub of foreign talk, and a child ran off to one of the caravans. From each of these, dark-skinned, dirty women came out, wrapped in vivid shawls and wearing gold earrings and necklaces of coins. Many were savagely handsome, and one after another they smiled, the leering, contemptuous smiles of beggars who know you can't get away without paying. One of them came forward, cringing round Maria, touching her fine London clothes with fingers that perhaps had never been washed since she was born.

"So you want your fortune told, pretty lady? You do not lack for money, lady, so it must be a matter of love?"

Maria looked round her, and every gypsy woman was mocking, but the men were still menacing.

"You must cross my palm with gold, pretty lady, if you want your fortune told. Gold brings luck."

Maria gave her a gold sovereign, thinking that this was cheaper than the other lady had had to pay for a dog. While she was opening her purse, they all drew a little nearer.

"Thank you, pretty lady. You shall see Mrs. Magda. She will tell you what you want to know—if you have enough to pay for it."

"You have five golden sovereigns in your purse, lady. That will be enough—if you are lucky. If Mrs. Magda likes you. Sometimes she will not."

"Where is she?"

"Her grandson will show you." She spoke to a small boy, and he ran ahead of them to a caravan painted yellow and red, where he put his head inside and gabbled in his foreign tongue.

"Come in, my dears," said a voice from inside.

They left the two footmen outside, looking nervous in a crowd of wild women. They stood stiffly and hoped they were impressive, but the gypsy women did not help them to feel it. They jabbered to each other, pointed, and laughed.

Inside, the caravan smelled like the monkeys' cage at the zoo, but worse. Garlic and onions and salt bacon and fish

169

hung from the roof, and there was a cage of budgereegahs and another of ferrets. Mrs. Magda was smoking a clay pipe. She was immensely fat, filling the whole of one bench. She was toothless and barefooted, but her greasy black hair had fancy combs stuck in it and her hands were swollen round her rings. She had the manner of a person who has everything she wants, including power.

"Sit down, pretty ladies. This is your lucky day. So there is something you want so much you will give old Magda five golden sovereigns to turn her inward eye upon it. You are wise, lady. It is little for much."

"I understood you sometimes do it for two."

"Lady! If it is only a question of a dog, you need not have disturbed my thoughts. I had not expected ladies to come heavily veiled for a dog. Max!"

Her grandson popped his head in.

"These ladies wish to go back. Tell your father there is no liberality in their hearts at all. My son hates a mean-fisted person, man or woman."

"No, no," said Maria. "I have come about something really important."

"Put your sovereigns then on the table, for the five points of the pentagon."

Maria did so.

"Give me those soft white hands."

Now gypsies move about the country and talk at the back door to servants and hang about fairs, and receive stolen goods from all and sundry and sell stolen poultry to dealers, and have eyes as sharp as foxes and ears as keen

170

as horses and memories as ready as their knives. So it was not altogether surprising that Mrs. Magda's first words were, as she held Maria's hand and rocked to and fro with closed eyes, "I smell burning. I see a great house in flames."

Maria's friend gave a gasp, and Mrs. Magda went on.

"I see a lovely lady in tears. She sits on one of her golden chairs in the garden that is red with fire and she weeps, and the young gentlemen can't comfort her."

Maria's hands trembled at the awful memory.

"But it is not the house she weeps for. Oh, no. Nor the silks and satins and costly laces all gone. Hidden in the house were the jewels that she was used to see round her own snow-white neck. Pretty lady! She weeps for her glittering beauty, her pearls cracked and blackened, her diamonds scattered in the rubbish, the red fire splitting her rubies."

"I knew they were in the house," Maria wailed. "Are they truly blackened and cracked—and scattered. Are they gone forever?"

Mrs. Magda gave a great snort and opened her eyes as if she was coming out of a trance. She peered at Maria with black eyes like a wicked hedgehog.

"The jewels!" Maria repeated. "Are they gone forever?"

"Forever is a long time, pretty lady. Not perhaps forever. They will be found. But you must be patient."

"What must I do?"

"Can you sew, pretty lady, with these fine fingers? You must have some hair from the head of every person

171

who was there, and with the hair you must embroider a picture of the house when the thief was in it, on that day. And with every stitch you must say: '*Great Moloch, Lord of Fire, put a pearl on this point.*'"

"What a dreadful thing to have to say! Wouldn't once do?"

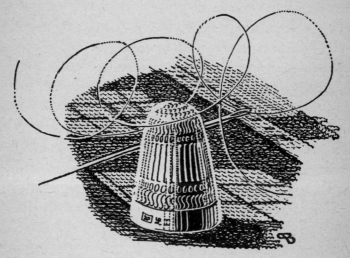

"With every stitch, pretty lady. Or there would be a pearl missing."

"What about the diamonds?"

"Take a different color of hair and say, '*Great Moloch, Lord of Fire, put a diamond on this point.*' And do not stop till you have done all the house, or there will be one corner where they might stay hidden."

The dirty paw with rings sunk in fat fingers came out and swept up the five sovereigns.

"Good day, pretty lady. May you be happy! Max!" The

old woman lit her pipe again and took no more notice of them except to nod when they said with trembling voices, "Thank you, Madame Magda."

They were glad to get into the fresh air, though the whole tribe was still there to be walked through, forty or fifty hostile mocking pairs of eyes, and not a word said.

When they reached the carriage, where several powerful-looking, slim-hipped gypsy men were standing, and no attack had yet been made, Maria lost her nerve. She emptied what was left in her purse on the grass to be scrambled for by the children, and climbing more like cats than ladies into the carriage, they were hardly seated before the coachman drove away at a gallop. It was not until they were safely away that Maria and her friend began to laugh.

"How frightened I was! My knees were shaking. But she must have second sight. I am sure of it. Every detail was right."

"Were you actually sitting in a gilt chair?"

"No. That was the Captain's mother. But still, it was very near. Now I remember her face. She looked as if she were praying to Moloch too. I hope she wasn't. I don't want any competition. She was certainly on the other side. Praying for everything to be burned."

"*She* hadn't paid five sovereigns."

"Six."

"Will you do what Mrs. Magda said?"

"Well, would not you? I admit it is tiresome to have to say such dreadful words. But still they can't mean anything. And if I get the jewels back, I needn't think about it any more."

So Maria settled down to make the picture. You can imagine that it took her a very long time. Think of Jacob's crinkly hair, hardly the length of a needle. The most she could do with it was tediously to make knots. Betsy undertook to get at least a hair of each of the staff. But then Caxton? Without him the picture would be useless, the spell wouldn't work. Luckily he was a vain man with hair he was proud of, and he had given a tress as a keepsake to Cook, who was persuaded to exchange it for a ring with which she could claim to have been secretly married to him. There was enough of Caxton's hair to do the whole chimney.

In and out went the needle in secret for two years and more, and with every stitch Maria said, "Great Moloch, Lord of Fire, put a pearl on this point." When the jewels still did not turn up, she remembered some detail to put in, still hoping. But perhaps she left something out or did it wrong, because the jewels never were found after all. Probably the gypsies had them all the time.

It was the last day. Tolly stood in front of the picture, which was the first thing in the house that he had noticed as being different when he came home for the holidays. There it was, and unless the gypsy was pretending, as Mrs. Oldknow had seemed to think, it had a secret. Tolly

174

looked searchingly for Jacob's hair, which must be blue-black. He decided it had been used for the eyes of the swans on the moat. Susan's was hazel brown—there was lots of that—and Maria's fair. There had been enough of Caxton's to do the old chimney. That could be a clue. Tolly leaned over the hearth and looked up it once again to the little square of sky. Jacob had climbed it, and Susan too in an emergency; and now after the winter's fires it was hung all the way up with thick soot like wool. And, he argued, Caxton could not have gone up it to hide something even on the nearest ledge without everybody noticing that he was black when he came down. Tolly was determined to go up it someday. Perhaps in the summer when he could do it in bathing trunks, like going up a cliff. And have a swim afterwards. After all, he had gone up the beech tree as high as Jacob did, which was as high as there was to go. He would never be content till he had looked out of the top of the chimney and called, "Hullo, Granny Partridge!"

For the moment, he decided to climb through the trap door in the ceiling of Jacob's closet and explore under the tiles, which he had never yet done. He did not find the extended and intricate space and the rows of arched stacks that Jacob had seen, because that had been burned down; but as he put his head through the trap door and shone his flashlight in, it looked large enough to be eerie. It had a sour smell not belonging to humans. The very first thing that crossed the beam of his flashlight was the largest spider he had ever seen, traveling slowly and purposefully on its hairy legs as if it watched him. The floor was not boarded, the space between the joists being filled in with a kind of sagging basketwork of slats and plaster, filled with dust, cobwebs, feathers, and the rubbish of old mouse nests. The space gave the impression of being much lived in by furtive creatures. It was not silent, as he had expected. There was a general faint rustling and ticking, and joists creaked where he was not treading. The tiles made a sounding board that magnified every noise. Above, in the open air, the roof had a regular population. Sparrows scrambled in the gutters, thrushes hammered snails, bees buzzed like a well-oiled machine. With his light trained on the floor, Tolly put a hand up to the sloping roof to steady himself. Instead of tiles his fingers met a vaguely living mass that moved with a sound like crumpled paper. He dropped to his knees with a scream and sprawled flat along a joint, losing his flashlight, for which he had to search with fear and disgust, moving his hands about among the litter till they found it again. Then with a great effort to be sensible, or at least to know the worst, he shone it on the tiles. For a moment he thought it was some kind of dried fungus, but it undoubtedly *squeaked*. Bats, a whole colony hanging upside down in close order, asleep. Tolly kept the light trained on them while he looked, to conquer his horror. One of them untucked its miniature foxlike head and yawned in his face, quite pretty, really. He wondered if Susan would like a bat, but remembering his sensation when he had first touched them, he left them alone.

The chimney stack was what he had come to examine.

It went up through the center of the house and was far bigger than he had imagined. What he had seen, looking up it from the living room, was only one flue, whereas the whole stack was a cluster of four. Each of these had its small iron door for the use of the sweep. Tolly edged round it, taking care not to put a foot through the ceiling. There was plenty of head room in the middle, so he need not fear putting his head into another bat colony. He opened one door—the catch he found was still broken— and peered up at the opening, still much farther away than he had expected. This was the living-room flue, the one Jacob had climbed. Next would be the downstairs room, then his great-grandmother's. Then his own. But here, built out on one side, there seemed to be an extra one that stopped short of the tiles in a rough edge, as if it had been scrapped before the new roof was put on—a narrow flue that had never been used since the fire. Which room did it go to? All the rooms now had fireplaces that were used. So it must go to *a room that wasn't there*. Tolly thought hard. Under his feet he knew was the music room, which he used to call the knight's hall because it went as high as the roof—as high as two rooms. Supposing once it had had a floor across it halfway up, making another attic bedroom like his own?

Supposing Caxton had slept there? He played his flashlight over the floor and found a framework that could have been a trap door, but the opening was filled with slat and plaster like all the rest. He knew it did not show on the ceiling of the music room. He opened the iron door of this flue with great difficulty. The latch was jammed or rusted together. When at last he succeeded by hammering it up with the heel of his shoe, the reason for its sticking was clear. A piece of rope was looped round the hook on the inside and dangled down out of sight. Tolly took hold of the rope. There was a weight on the end of it, and something made sharp dragging sounds against the wall of the flue.

Nothing had frightened him as much as this. The first thought that came into his head was that Caxton had hanged himself—that on the end of the rope was a skeleton. When he pulled on the rope, its face would come up grinning with teeth. He leaned against the chimney and felt very peculiar. Then he tried to think. A skeleton, he supposed—he had never met one—would rattle. He dared to put his hand in again and swing the rope. It made again a dragging sound and a muffled clinking. A skeleton of course might have clothes on. A coat would last a long time. The weight as far as he could judge was frighteningly right. Tolly was numb with terror, his tongue dry and his knees shaking, but curiosity made his hands pull on the rope whether he meant to or not, and whatever was on the end came dragging nearer. At last something vaguely like a brown hairy head covered thickly with soot appeared, with the rope tied round its neck. Tolly screamed as loud as his dry mouth could before he saw that it was the neck of a sack, unmistakably the neck of a sack, nothing more or less. He hauled it out, dragged it to the open trap door, and lowered it into the closet, calling at the top of his voice for his great-grandmother.

She happened to be in the music room underneath, listening with amusement to his feet overhead. When she heard his first squeal as he put his hand among the bats, she smiled to herself. She always enjoyed his instant imagination. But when she heard the strangled nightmare screech that greeted his first sight of the sack, she hurried up the attic stairs very fast indeed for an old lady, arriving all concern just as he dragged his sack out into the room.

"What happened, Tolly? I was afraid you had hurt yourself."

"It was worse than that," he gasped, but could not say what, because the mere memory made him stammer. His face was so excited that he looked, she thought, like someone talking in delirium. He was struggling with the knot in the rope.

"Look what I've found. It was in Caxton's chimney. I'm sure it's right. It's *them*."

He freed the neck of the sack and plunged his arm in up to the shoulder. He brought out a green baize bag, motheaten, with silver spoons half falling out of the holes. "That was the bones," he said. Then came a canvas bag, much heavier, from which he feverishly spilled out golden sovereigns that rolled and spun over the floor, twinkling in the shafts of sun. A few of them slipped down cracks and were lost as soon as found. But there were hundreds. They were under Tolly's bed and under the rocking horse and sticking half out from under his trunk and making haphazard patterns all over the polished floor, besides those

179

piled like a sand heap between his palms, their ribbed edges electrifying his skin and pleasing his eyes.

They were both silent, looking at each other with bright eyes.

"What lovely little things they are," she said at last. "We'd better take a good look. We shall never see this room with a drift of golden sovereigns again. Let's just leave them there for the present while we empty the sack. There is something in it still."

Tolly pulled out a small bundle, which was wrapped in a shirt, the sleeves crossed over and tied, the lace cuffs making a fancy bow as on a box of chocolates.

"Don't be so reckless this time," said Mrs. Oldknow, spreading Tolly's face towel on the floor. "Though of course it may be only farthings. Or only tobacco."

The shirt was spread out. "It's one of Sefton's," said Tolly, recognizing it from the patchwork. Inside the shirt was a yellow-and-black apron tied again with the strings. Mrs. Oldknow sat down suddenly. "Really, I never knew opening parcels could be such a strain."

And there they were—the pearls, the diamonds, the rubies, the earrings, the bracelets, and the brooches, all jumbled up together.

As Tolly drew up out of the heap the necklace of diamonds, the strings of pearls slithered down its length like water over rocks and easily detached themselves. Only the hard stones tangled and caught in their settings and hung tightly onto bracelets. Tolly separated each piece and hung them one by one on his great-grandmother till she was festooned with glitter, her fingers stiff with rings, her ears rattling with earrings. On her head he put an ornament like a curled fern made of emeralds.

"You do look funny! Not like yourself at all. You look like the oldest of all witch doctors come to do very special Juju. I wish Jacob could see you. And you see, the gypsy *was* right. Her magic really worked."

"I suppose," said Mrs. Oldknow regretfully, "we *ought* to gather up the sovereigns before lunch. It doesn't seem quite right to leave them there, not quite respectful. What a morning!"

"Now you won't have to sell the picture," said Tolly proudly as they went in for lunch. Then he stopped, astounded. "Why, Granny, there it is!"

Maria's picture had been taken down, and in its place hung the beloved oil painting of Toby with his deer, Alexander, Linnet, their mother, their grandmother, the chaffinch, and the little black-and-white dog. Tolly was delighted.

"Why, how did you get it back so soon?"

"I thought it would be a surprise for you on your last day. The exhibition is over, and though somebody wanted to buy the picture, I couldn't bear to let it go at once. So I said I would think about it. Wasn't that lucky! Suppose I had sold it and then you had found the jewels. We couldn't have got it back."

"I *am* glad to see them again." Tolly moved round the table to see if their eyes still followed him, and of course they did, all five pairs of them.

181

It was a meal with more chatter and laughter than eating. What a lot of things they could do now! The roof could be mended. They could go to Cornwall for the summer.

"There are only three real sailing ships left in the world, but I know someone in Falmouth who could take you over the *Cutty Sark*." Tolly could have—what did he want most on earth, after a thoroughbred? He'd have to wait for that.

"If I had a tape recorder, do you think I could catch voices—*theirs*, I mean?"

"There's no knowing. It might come out a real babel, all of them, all at once. A unique 'historical party.' "

"I suppose I must take all that to the bank. I daren't keep it here."

"Where have you put the jewels now?"

"I tied them up again in the shirt. Didn't know what else to do with such things."

"Will you take them to the bank like that? Wouldn't an egg basket with a sheet of paper over the top be better?"

"The bank will expect a suitcase for decency."

"Aren't you going to keep anything for yourself?"

"Yes. Do you see the big brooch that Linnet's mother is wearing in the picture?"

"Why, that's among the ones we found."

"Of course. They are all family jewels. And Linnet's little string of pearls that Maria kept from Susan. Yes, I must certainly allow myself the luxury of keeping some."

Tolly went with her to the bank, carrying the suitcase that contained what no one could imagine. If he expected the bank to be excited, he was disappointed. The manager was respectful in the presence of money. He did say a few words about the gold sovereigns and the dates on them, that was all. They were counted into piles, and then, with the jewels, which were put each in a separate green baize bag, laid in an iron box and shut up in the massive safe.

"Well, really," said his great-grandmother as they came out together. "It may be sensible, but isn't it a dull way to treat them! Do you know, I really prefer Caxton's sack."

And now it was nearly the end of the very last day. Tolly went into the garden. Almost no time left, he thought. Four hours, three hours, two hours, one hour—even in the last minute something might happen. Why do people only invent things that go faster and faster, instead of finding some way to keep it at now? The moor hen was softly clucking on the moat to warn her chicks that someone was there. The house robin perched on a twig by Tolly's ear and, looking him in the eye, made a few twitters that must have been felt as pinches by the worm in his beak. Then he dived into his nest in the ivy. Tolly stood still to hear the nestlings' greedy squeaks, and as the robin flew away again, he heard Susan's voice.

"I'll put it on."

She and Jacob were kneeling by the Green Deer. Jacob's head was in a turbaned bandage. He had apparently been teaching her to make garlands, and she was putting one round the Green Deer's neck.

"Why did you never bring me a real deer, Jacob, as I asked you to?" Susan was exacting.

"Ai, Miss Susan, how can I get a real deer unless I poach like Fred, but far away, in King's park? Miss Susan ask for elephant too."

"I terribly want a real deer." She stroked its leafy neck. "It's only a bush," she said.

Tolly felt someone looking at him, and lifting his eyes, saw Toby standing on the far side of Susan and Jacob, about the same distance from them as himself. Tolly exchanged with him the look of old friends. The other two seemed unaware of them.

"Toby, call your deer."

Toby grinned and gave a low singing call.

A little wind ruffled the Green Deer's back, which seemed at its touch to grow softer. It wrinkled up, twitched at the shoulder as if a fly had lit there, and while Susan's hands round it were motionless in astonishment, the deer moved its handsome ears in Toby's direction, stretched its neck this way and that as if stiff from sleep, and licked Susan's hand.

"Jacob! Jacob! The real deer is here. It licked me."

"Ai, Missy!" Jacob's voice came sadly through the garden where Tolly was again alone.

"You blind, but you see things sometimes when I can't."

The robin was back again with another worm, and the nestlings' clamor was imprudent in such absolute silence.

The school clothes were assembled, the trunks packed,

184

the tuck box roped. Tolly was in bed, and there was nothing left but one night in his own bed and tomorrow's unhappy breakfast.

His great-grandmother sat on his bed.

"What happened to Susan in the end, Granny?"

"She married Jonathan and lived happily ever after, and had lots of children who could all see."

"And then what happened to Jacob?"

"When Jacob was thirteen, the Captain apprenticed him to the groom, to be trained as Susan's own, to drive her and look after her and her horses, and to take her riding pillion when they didn't use the carriage. And when Susan and Jonathan went on their honeymoon, the Captain took Jacob in the *Woodpecker* on a voyage to Barbados, where he chose himself a wife from his own people and brought her back with him. And he lived happily too. His wife was Nanny to Susan's children, and he and Susan were always devoted friends. As for the children, whether black or white, they could never leave him alone. He grew into a very big man, and they loved him as much as you would love a gentle, playful lion."